In a Small Town

Debby Fowler

A Felicity Paradise crime novel

ISBN 978 185022 238 5

Published by Truran, Goonance, Water Lane,
St Agnes, Cornwall TR5 0RA
www.truranbooks.co.uk

Truran is an imprint of Truran Books Ltd

www.felicityparadise.com

The paper used for this publication has been produced
from trees that have been legally sourced from well-
managed and credibly certifiied forests.

Printed and bound in Cornwall by R. Booth Ltd,
The Praze, Penryn, TR10 8AA

For Alan.
Thank you for all your support over the years

PROLOGUE

West Cornwall, October 2009

He was not a bad lad. Indeed, if Becky's parents had ever had the chance to meet him, they probably would have thought he was the sort of young man she should marry. He was of medium height, medium build with medium brown hair, he was moderately good-looking but not in a flamboyant way. What saved him from being nondescript were his eyes, not their colour which was hazel, but the fact that they twinkled with mischief and laughter, reminiscent of the little boy he had been so recently. Despite his youth, there were already the beginnings of laughter lines around his eyes because he laughed so easily and readily, because he loved life.

However, an exuberant love of life can be a dangerous weapon in the wrong hands. After a series of carefully-nurtured old bangers which had seen him through college and university, Harry Stephens had just taken possession of a brand-new car with that brand-new car smell, and any number of gadgets.

He had joined the A30 at St Ives and once clear of the Hayle roundabout, he took the car up to eighty with so little effort and noise it was hard to believe he was travelling so fast.

'Remember the big dipper, Harry,' said Becky, putting her hand on his knee.

'I will,' said Harry, slowing down as they approached the great sweep of road which took them steeply down hill and then up the other side in a 60-mile-an-hour limit. Then they were on the dual carriageway again heading towards Truro. It was pitch dark although it was only early evening, the late October nights drawing in fast. Wisps of mist laid fingers across the road.

'I love this car,' Harry sang out.

'Are you sure you're happy to drive tonight, Harry?' said a voice behind him. 'I don't mind not drinking and it would give me a chance to try out this new toy of yours.'

'Not a chance, Miles,' Harry said. 'It was a bit of a heavy night last night, wasn't it? A few pints of orange juice tonight will do me no harm at all. Besides no one gets to drive this baby but me, not yet anyway.'

The wall of fog suddenly dropped in front of them like a curtain.

'Shit,' said Harry. He slowed a little and flipped on his fog lights but stayed in the fast lane.

'It's what Dad would call a real pea-souper,' said Becky. 'I think you should slow down, Harry.'

'It's OK,' said Harry, 'I can see where I'm going, I'll stay in the fast lane, it's the safest. Find us some music, Becky, it'll help me to concentrate.'

Becky started twisting the dials. 'I can't find Pirate FM,' she complained.

'It's all pre-tuned,' said Harry, irritably. 'You shouldn't have a problem, don't fiddle about, just press the buttons.' He glanced at her. 'Seriously Becky, don't mess it up, I spent ages getting it just as I wanted it.'

He had only taken his eyes off the road for a second but when he returned his attention to the road there was a looming shape, a cattle lorry, ahead of him overtaking an old van. It was only feet away. He jammed his foot hard onto the brake pedal, not used to the responses of a new car. The ensuing swerve took him into the crash barrier. There was the sound of screaming metal, of screaming Becky, and then he bounced off the barrier and careered across the road into the path of an ancient Volvo he had passed moments before without even seeing it. The Volvo was being driven by Margaret Berry, a

56-year-old widow, on her way to visit her brand-new grandson at the Royal Cornwall Hospital, a grandson she would now never see.

The first on the scene was Sergeant Jack Curnow. He and a young constable, Mike Freeman, were on their way back to Truro following enquiries they had been making in Penzance. There had been a drugs bust the week before and there were still a lot of unanswered questions. They had the riff-raff under lock and key but they were little more than victims themselves. The main protagonists, however, were still at large.

'I'll ask around,' Jack Curnow had said to his boss, Chief Inspector Penrose.

'Take someone with you,' his boss had said, 'but I tell you now, it will be a complete waste of time, like getting blood out of a stone.'

He had been right.

It was a scene of carnage. Jack called for back-up and when Mike Freeman had finished throwing up, he put him on to directing traffic, a dangerous business in this fog – there would be more trouble if they weren't careful. It was a dodgy situation. A quick inspection of the tangled metal, which had once been two cars, convinced Jack that no one could have survived the crash. Minutes later though, when the paramedics were on the scene, a shout went up.

'We've got a live one here; we need to get him out fast.'

Jack ran back to the wreckage. The traffic was now in the hands of the police. A paramedic was on his hands and knees peering through what had once been a car window. 'I've put a line into him but we need to move him fast, he's losing a lot of blood.'

Jack knelt down on the road. The paramedic had set up a lantern to work by and Jack found himself gazing at the face of a young man who was vaguely familiar, although he couldn't place him. His face was unmarked apart from a thin trickle of blood that seemed to be coming from a very superficial-looking wound at the temple, but his features were twisted with pain.

'What's your name, son?' Jack asked gently.

'Miles,' he replied. 'Miles Irving.'

1

November 2009, Truro

For a moment Chief Inspector Keith Penrose sat gawping like a schoolboy at the beautiful girl standing before him, then his natural good manners propelled him to his feet. He came around from behind his desk, extending a hand.

'Keith Penrose,' he said.

The girl took his hand and smiled at him. 'You don't remember me, do you?' she said.

Keith frowned. He was good with names and faces, had to be in his job, but as far as he was concerned, he had never seen this girl before in his life. 'I'm struggling,' he admitted.

The girl laughed and let go of his hand. 'I'm glad,' she said. 'I feel a different person; I *am* a different person.' She spoke with a slight accent he couldn't place. 'Shall I put you out of your misery?' she asked.

'I think you'd better; come and sit down.' The girl looked bewildered. There was nowhere to sit; the two chairs on the visitors' side of the desk were piled high with files. 'Sorry,' said Keith, picking up one of the piles and dropping them clumsily to the floor, 'take a seat.' The girl did as she was told and waited while Keith retreated behind his desk. 'Well?' he asked, once he too was seated.

'My name is Anya Cascescu.'

'Of course it is,' Keith said, 'of course it is, but I would never have known, you are…' He hesitated, trying to find the right words. 'You are looking truly wonderful.' His thoughts slipped back to the first time he had met Anya. She had been a child prostitute brought over from Romania, and he had found a Romanian priest to act as an interpreter while he interviewed her. She had stayed the night in Felicity Paradise's house having been found on the Harbour Beach. Anya's harrowing tale had shocked them all to the core… and now look at her!

'You must wonder why I've come to see you,' Anya said, breaking into his thoughts. 'Two reasons, firstly I wanted to thank you – it is through you I have a home and a family.'

Keith's mind struggled with the details of the four-year-old case. 'You went to live with some friends of my daughter's, the Roberts, wasn't it, near

Bodmin?'

'Yes, that's right, and after the court case you kindly wrote to the immigration authorities on my behalf. I'm sure it helped a great deal because I am a British citizen now. I am very grateful.'

'I'm so glad and have you been happy with the Roberts family?'

'Oh yes, they've been wonderful to me. It was my twenty-first birthday last week, they gave a huge party for me, they are so kind.'

'Twenty-one!' Keith said. 'How time flies, congratulations Anya.'

'Thank you,' she smiled warmly at him.

She really was glorious to behold with high cheek bones, deep brown almond-shaped eyes, a beautifully clear complexion and long dark glossy hair. The tiny half-starved waif had become tall too, tall and willowy. The transformation was extraordinary.

'Thank you, not only for your good wishes,' said Anya, 'but thank you too for helping to turn my life around.'

'I didn't do much,' Keith murmured, 'but I have thought about you often and wondered how you were getting on. I should have contacted you before, but time, pressure, work…' He shrugged.

'I didn't expect to hear from you again,' Anya reassured him, 'but you were there for me when I needed it, that's what is important.'

'So what are you doing with your life now?' Keith asked.

'I'm still living with the Roberts although I am now officially grown up,' she smiled. 'I did childcare at Truro College so as well as helping with the Roberts children, I help out with the children from two other families in the area – after school, that sort of thing. I love it, I love the work, I love children.'

'And no doubt you'll have some of your own one day,' Keith said, thoughtlessly.

A cloud passed across Anya's beautiful face. 'I don't have to pretend to you, Chief Inspector, you know my background. I can't ever imagine there ever being a man in my life, a boyfriend, not after …' Her voice trailed away.

'You are still that damaged?' Keith asked her gently.

Anya nodded. 'I think so, I can't ever see myself, well, being with a man, wanting to be with a man.'

'Maybe one day,' said Keith, 'the right man, a gentle man in every way.'

Anya shrugged. 'It's about a man that I've come to see you,' she said, 'as well as to say thank you. I've been feeling guilty about him and then suddenly there was his name in the paper.'

Keith eyed her shrewdly. 'You're talking about Miles Irving, aren't you?'

Anya nodded. 'Is he alright? The paper said he had been severely injured in that car crash.'

'I've been to see him a couple of times in hospital,' Keith said, 'and he is making good progress. He very nearly lost a leg, and now he may always have a limp I think, but they managed to save it. Miles is a musician, did you know that?' Anya shook her head. 'He plays the violin like an angel apparently and mercifully his fingers and arms came out unscathed from the crash. He is very lucky to be alive.'

'I wanted to talk to you about him,' said Anya, 'because I wondered whether he would like me to tell him about his sister, Marianna, you know, what she was like, the little things.'

'How long did you know Marianna?' Keith asked.

'Not that long really,' said Anya, 'we were both girls who had escaped from orphanages but we were not in the same orphanage. We…' she hesitated, 'we met on the streets of Bucharest. I was only twelve and Marianna, she looked after me, taught me how to survive. When she heard there was this opportunity to work in England in domestic service, she said she would not go unless I could come too. Of course she wasn't to know that it was a trick.

The first few months in England were terrible, worse even than Bucharest. She felt so guilty for bringing me here but once I came to Cornwall and my life changed around, I realised how much I owed Marianna. I just wish she hadn't had to die.' Anya's eyes filled with tears.

'I can see you'd like to tell Miles about his sister, but do you feel it will help him to hear the awful things she suffered?'

Anya shook her head vigorously. 'Of course I don't want to tell him about our lives, I tell no one about that ever, it was too…' Words failed her. 'But I want to tell him about Marianna, the person, how good she was, how kind, how funny. I've thought about it often. They only met for a few minutes before she was killed, he can't have got to know her at all. I thought maybe…'

'You thought maybe it was time?' Keith suggested gently.

'Yes,' said Anya, 'but I will be guided by you, Chief Inspector. I won't go to see him unless you think it is a good idea.'

'I do think it is a good idea,' said Keith, 'but what I think I should do first is prepare the ground, tell him that you would like to see him and see how he reacts. He is a very complex character with a lot of issues; this prolonged stay in hospital, and his friends dying in the crash, has made him even more introspective. Personally, I believe a visit from you is just what he needs but I think probably I should check it out first. What do you say?'

'I agree,' said Anya, 'I don't want to go marching into his life and cause him any more unhappiness.'

From his vantage point, three floors above the car park, Keith watched Anya walk away from the building; she had the natural elegance of a model. What an extraordinary turn-around and yet clearly she was still deeply damaged. What would a meeting between her and Miles do for each of them – dig up issues from their grisly past certainly but would it soothe or upset them? It was impossible to tell.

He turned away from the window and sat down heavily behind his desk. The plight of Miles, his sister Marianna and little Anya brought to mind, not only their trials and tribulations, but he was ashamed to realise, the thought of Felicity Paradise. He and Felicity had not seen each other for nearly a year. It was by mutual consent: they didn't trust themselves to be together. They had spoken briefly on the phone, but there was so much Keith wanted to tell her and he realised suddenly that the visit of Anya had given him the perfect excuse. Felicity had a natural instinct, particularly where the young were concerned. She would know whether it was a good thing for Anya and Miles to meet. He lifted the phone, his natural good humour restored. He dialled the familiar number and waited. As he did so, he pictured her house in his mind; the phone was in the kitchen with its cosy Aga, two Windsor chairs positioned either side of it, French windows leading out onto the balcony with its stunning views across St Ives harbour. The phone cut to answerphone, Felicity informing him that she was not in and he should leave a message. He listened to her voice like some lovesick teenager, then replaced the receiver and fished around in his suit pocket for his mobile.

She answered on the second ring. 'Chief Inspector, how lovely to hear from you.'

'How are you,' he said, 'come to that, *where* are you? It sounds very noisy.'

'Actually, I'm in Truro buying socks in M and S, all mine have gone into holes at the same moment. Sorry, sorry, too much information, you don't need to know about my footwear problems.'

'On the contrary,' Keith replied, 'a problem shared and all that.'

She laughed. 'What can I do for you?'

'Well, actually I was hoping for some advice,' Keith said. He hesitated. 'I suppose as you're in Truro, you wouldn't like to meet for a drink or a coffee?'

There was a moment's silence. 'I suppose we could,' Felicity said, cautiously.

'Only if it is convenient,' Keith hurried on, 'it's about little Anya, you remember little Anya Cascescu, the Romanian girl?'

'Of course I remember Anya,' Felicity cut in. 'She's not in trouble, is she?'

'She's fine, in fact wonderful. Look, what about Mannings in half an hour, will that give you time to sort out your sock problem?'

'I should hope so,' said Felicity, 'I'll see you there.'

2

Felicity Paradise was looking very good. Her hair was cut short and tousled; it suited her, made her look younger. As usual she was dressed in vibrant eccentric colours, purple trousers and a baggy striped jumper sporting all the colours of the rainbow. She smiled broadly at Keith as she approached the table and he stood up awkwardly to greet her. Briefly he took her hand and kissed her carefully on the cheek. Her hand in his trembled slightly; they separated quickly and sat down at opposite sides of the little table.

'I took the precaution of getting you a dry white wine, the sun being over the yard arm. I hope that's the right thing.'

'I should say so,' said Felicity. 'You look well.'

'So do you,' he said, 'stunning as always.'

'Sorry about the jumper,' said Felicity, 'it is a bit over the top, only I love it.'

'Successful sock buying?'

Felicity waved a Marks and Spencer carrier bag

at him triumphantly. 'Hugely successful.'

'I like the new hair, and you're thinner.' He knew he shouldn't be talking like this.

'It's all the dog walking,' said Felicity, 'I've been doing a lot of that lately, marching around on the cliff path. Harvey has lost weight too. For a Jack Russell he was starting to look a little portly. It's because I spoil him – him being an only child.'

'Hardly only,' said Keith. 'How's the family?'

'Really good,' said Felicity, 'both children are still happily married, no small achievement these days, and the grandchildren are all flourishing. And yours?'

'OK,' said Keith, 'but rather spread out at the moment. Will has a job in Germany stripping out and refurbishing luxury yachts, it's not really what he wants to do, he really wants to build from new, but it is a good start and he'll learn a lot. I think he was starting to get cabin fever in West Cornwall, it is a bit parochial after travelling around with the army.'

'I can well imagine,' said Felicity, 'and does he have a girlfriend?'

Keith shook his head. 'Not at the moment, well, not one he is admitting to anyway.'

'And Carly?'

'She and her boyfriend Graham have…' Keith hesitated, a look of pain crossing his face. 'They've gone to Australia, to Sydney. Graham has a job at the university there, you know he's a marine biologist?' Felicity nodded. 'And Carly has walked straight into a job at one of the hospitals as a physio. They are loving it.'

'And you wish they weren't?' Felicity took a sip of her wine. 'Delicious, thank you.'

'How can I not be pleased for them?' Keith said. 'They have job security, sunshine, and a healthy lifestyle. Carly says living over there is so much easier than here. They're not earning any more money, but it seems to go much further. She says it is all so simple – entertaining your friends involves taking a crate of beer onto the beach and barbecuing. Being a Cornish girl, she has always loved surfing and now she is in her element.'

'There is a wistful note to your voice, Chief Inspector. Do you think she may not come back?'

'I wouldn't, if I was her,' Keith said.

'You could visit,' said Felicity.

'Oh I know but it's just not the same as Carly dropping in for Sunday lunch, is it?'

'How is your wife, is she alright?' Felicity asked.

'Yes but a little nervous about her job. Streamlining all the individual councils into one Cornwall Council inevitably means some job losses.'

'She is quite senior though, isn't she, in

Planning?'

Keith nodded. 'Yes, but cuts are going to have to be made and you know the old adage, the higher you climb the further you fall. I honestly don't know if her fears are justified but she is certainly feeling insecure. Are you working at the moment?'

'I'm still working at the school, two days a week now, and I still look after my grandchildren for another two days a week and on the remaining days I paint. I've had a couple of small commissions for children's book illustrations and I've started selling my own cards. It's going rather well.'

'Really, how does that work?'

'I'm very unambitious at the moment,' said Felicity. 'I've just painted a few slightly quirky scenes of St Ives. An insurance policy came up just over a year ago, not much money but a bit, and I've used some of it to have the cards printed. I'm just selling them locally at the moment in St Ives and Penzance, a few here in Truro too. They're selling really well. I'm also selling a few paintings with the same sort of theme.'

'Good for you,' said Keith.

Felicity smiled at him. 'It's not a mighty enterprise but it just about keeps Harvey in Bonios. Now, tell me about Anya.'

Keith leaned back in his chair.

'She came to see me this morning. She looks

absolutely wonderful, stunning. She has British citizenship and is still living in Bodmin with Carly's chums but she has worked up a little business looking after children. She seemed…' he hesitated, 'confident, happy, content.'

'Has she a boyfriend?' Felicity asked.

'I asked that. I think it is going to be a long time before there is a man in her life.'

'Not surprising,' said Felicity, quietly.

'Anyway,' said Keith, 'the reason for her visit is that she had read about Miles's accident in *The Cornishman*. You must have read about it. You remember Miles, don't you? She wondered whether it would be helpful to him if she talked to him about his sister. She and Marianna were together for three years, and they got to know each other very well. Marianna was like a mother to her she said.'

'Oh, that poor boy,' said Felicity. 'Firstly, nobody tells him he is adopted; then when his long-lost sister finds him and tells him the truth about his birth, she is murdered; then he finds the body… and now this, a horrendous car crash in which he lost his friends. How badly is he injured? How is he?'

'He's different,' said Keith, 'different from the boy he was when we were investigating Marianna's murder. He's older, of course, but there is a coldness, a hardness about him that there wasn't before. He's very cynical and he's toughened up a lot. Whether that's a good thing or not, I'm not sure. What do you think? Do you think he'd benefit from meeting Anya?'

Felicity hesitated. 'It's going to rake up everything again, but then it can never be far below the surface of his thoughts, not something as horrific as that. I'd have thought it would be helpful and while he is stuck in hospital down here, a good opportunity too. How about Anya, do you think Anya can cope with Miles?'

'She knows he is very damaged, as is she,' said Keith, thoughtfully. 'It might be possible that they could help each other or maybe they will find that what they have to tell each other is too painful. Anya is no fool and she is well aware of the sensitivity of the situation. She promised me that she would not be too graphic about the life she and Marianna led. She wants to tell him about Marianna, the person. I truly believe her only motive for meeting Miles is to try and help him.'

'Why has she left it so long?' Felicity asked.

'I imagine her first priority was to sort out herself. You remember what a poor little waif she was when we first met her; abused mentally, physically, psychologically and drug-dependent – she's unrecognisable as that person now, but she must have had to work very hard to put herself back together. As she explained things to me, it was

Miles's accident which triggered the thought in her mind that maybe she owed it to him to tell him as much as she could about his sister. I imagine also, there was a practical element to it. Miles lives in London normally and here he is stuck in Cornwall for weeks on end while his leg mends.'

'You'll clearly have to tell Miles that Anya would like to meet him,' Felicity said, after a brief silence. Keith nodded. 'The question is whether you are going to encourage him to see her.'

'I rather think I am, aren't I?' Keith asked.

'I rather think you are,' Felicity agreed.

The mid-afternoon traffic heading out towards the hospital was heavy. Keith, anxious to keep his mind from dwelling on Felicity Paradise, used the time to recall the details of the Irving case. It had been a strange one – of history repeating itself. Identical twin brothers, separated shortly after birth, one adopted, the other left neglected in a bleak post-war children's home. The former became a top industrialist, the latter a gardener on Tresco; the former a ruthless bully, the latter a gentle, shy recluse. The industrialist, Sir Hugo Irving adopted a son of his own, separating him from his sister as he himself had been separated from his brother.

Extraordinary, more the stuff of fiction, except that it wasn't, it had truly happened. Then, if that wasn't enough, to spice things up, along came MI5 with the suggestion that Sir Hugo was a spy, possibly a double agent, working for Russia as well as the UK... or maybe not, it was never clear. Then there was a death, but which brother had been murdered? Officially it was Sir Hugo but Keith had always believed the true victim had been Hugo's gentle brother Bob. Either way the case was closed on the orders of Keith's boss. Intriguingly, Miles had to know who he was living with, his father or his uncle and so did Sir Hugo's alleged widow. It was a mess, one Keith would clearly have loved to unravel but orders from on high had prevented him from doing so. The temptation to ask Miles to tell him the truth was very great, but so far he had resisted it. He had a soft spot for Miles, even with this new veneer of toughness.

Keith was in a thoroughly bad temper by the time he reached Miles Irving's bedside. The car park for the Treliske Hospital was totally inadequate in terms of size. Finding a car parking space was considered to be akin to winning the National Lottery. Amazingly Keith had found a space after only five or six circuits of the car park. He made his way through the bleak hospital corridors to Miles's ward only to be told that the previous day Miles had been transferred to the private Duchy Hospital down the road. To make matters worse this piece of information had been delivered to Keith with evident satisfaction by the receptionist, who clearly took great pleasure in his frustration. He had then got lost twice extricating himself from the hospital, only to find that he had no change for the pay machine and so had to retrace his steps and buy a chocolate bar he didn't want from the hospital shop.

The Duchy Hospital was a much more civilised affair. There was parking space, no charge and he was in Miles's private room within two to three minutes.

'You might have told me you were moving hospitals,' Keith said, flinging himself into the visitor's chair.

Miles smiled at him. 'And good afternoon to you too, Chief Inspector.'

Keith met his eye and smiled. 'Sorry, how are you? You look a bit better I think.'

With his narrow frame, shock of black hair and huge brown eyes, Miles looked more like twelve than the 22 he was, but the greenish complexion that had accompanied his first few days in hospital had definitely gone, though he was still very pale with dark smudges under his eyes.

'It's less painful,' Miles said, indicating his leg, 'but I'm going to be stuck here for another couple of weeks at least, possibly three, depending how it heals. Mother tried to have me moved up to London by private ambulance, would you believe. I put my foot down metaphorically speaking. I prefer being in Cornwall in this funny little hospital.'

'Standing up to your mother, that was brave of you,' Keith said, memories of Lady Irving and her formidable nature coming back to him from the various interviews he had conducted with her regarding the disappearance of her husband.

'Yes, it was rather,' Miles agreed. 'So, to what do I owe the pleasure Chief Inspector – do you want to ask me some more about the crash?' A look of pain crossed his face.

Keith shook his head, hurriedly. 'No, no, this is more of a social call.'

'Wow!' said Miles, 'I am honoured.'

'That's enough, my boy,' Keith said and they smiled at one another affectionately. Keith, well aware he was treading on sensitive ground, plunged straight in. 'I had a visit this morning from a very beautiful young woman.'

'Lucky you' said Miles, 'more than I've had. I would have thought you were getting rather too old for that sort of thing.'

Keith ignored the quip. 'Her name is Anya Cascescu, she is the girl who came over to England with your sister , the one with whom Marianna was particularly friendly. It was Anya who followed her down to Cornwall.'

Miles instantly sobered. 'I know who Anya is,' he said, quietly.

'She's done really well,' said Keith. 'She has been virtually adopted by a farming family in Bodmin – they're friends of my daughter. She has British citizenship now and has developed a career looking after children. She's unrecognisable from the poor little creature we found on the beach in St Ives.'

'I'm glad,' said Miles, simply.

There was a pause. 'The thing is,' said Keith, 'she'd like to meet you.'

Miles immediately shook his head. 'I don't think so.'

'Wait,' said Keith, 'just hear me out, will you?' Miles nodded slightly. 'I know there are aspects of your sister's life you can't bear to hear about but Anya is a very sensitive girl, she doesn't want to meet you to tell you the horrors of her life or Marianna's. She just wants to tell you about the sort of person your sister was, she loved your sister, she says your sister was like a mother to her. She is well aware that you and Marianna hardly met and she just thought it would be helpful to tell you a little bit about the kind of person she was. There is no ulterior motive, I'm sure of it.'

'I don't think I can bear it,' said Miles, 'when I think about the privileged life I've led and the type of life Marianna had to endure, I don't think I could face up to the reality of what she went through. I've dealt with it by blocking it out these last few years.'

'It wasn't your fault, Miles,' Keith said, gently. 'For whatever reason your parents decided to adopt you but not your sister, it was they who caused the split, not you.'

'It was because of Elizabeth,' Miles said.

Keith frowned. 'Remind me, who is Elizabeth?'

'My parents had a child by birth before I was born. Her name was Elizabeth. She had a congenital heart problem, she died when she was very young, two or three. I'm not sure whether they couldn't have any more children or did not dare risk a repeat of the condition. Either way, that's why they went to Romania to adopt a baby. When they found me and Marianna sharing a cot in Orphanage Number One, they couldn't take Marianna – at least that's what my mother told me – because she was exactly the age as Elizabeth would have been had she lived. They couldn't bear the concept of trying to replace their daughter.'

'If one is being compassionate,' said Keith, 'trying to see it from their point of view, you can understand where they were coming from.'

'You think it's justified to split up siblings like that?' Miles said, angrily.

Keith met his eye. 'No,' he said, 'I don't. They had plenty of money and an enormous house, there would have been no problem taking two children rather than one, but I think you have to understand what they were doing in adopting you.'

'Which was what?' Miles asked.

Keith stood up and started restlessly striding around the room. 'I've no right to voice an opinion,' he said, 'I've been so lucky, I have two children of my own which my wife managed to conceive without any problems. Who am I to play judge and jury?'

'Just say what you were going to say,' Miles said.

Keith stopped his pacing. 'They went to Romania to adopt a baby to fulfil their needs, not the needs of the baby. They had lost a child, they were devastated, and as you say, they either couldn't or dared not risk having another. Therefore, when they found you and your sister in the orphanage, they weren't thinking about you and her as a family in your own right, they were simply looking for a baby who very obviously wasn't a replacement for Elizabeth. You were of a different sex and age, you fitted the bill just fine, Marianna didn't.'

'So you're saying they just went shopping –

shopping for a baby,' Miles said, bitterly.

'No, I'm saying that grief is a funny thing,' said Keith. 'Of all the emotions we humans put ourselves through, I think grief can warp one's judgement more than any other.'

'More than love?' Miles asked.

'I think its effect is more subtle,' Keith said. 'We're used to the terminology "blinded by love" and that is certainly true – one ignores the realities of the beloved or the inappropriateness of the loving. Grief is different – it warps a person's outlook without them realising. Your parents needed the emotional fulfilment of a baby who wasn't Elizabeth and that was their primary objective.' He shrugged and smiled at Miles. 'It's only an opinion, I'm probably way off beam, but one thing's for sure, the fact that Marianna was left behind and had to endure the life that she did is no fault of yours, you have to admit that.'

'It doesn't stop me feeling guilty and miserable about it,' Miles said.

'My mother always said that guilt was self-indulgence,' Keith said.

'Really,' said Miles, 'how does that work?'

'Well, I suppose guilt is only one step away from self-pity, isn't it?' said Keith. 'Wallowing in guilt instead of trying to do something about putting things right.'

'I can't put things right though, can I?' said Miles, bitterly. 'My sister is dead, I can't bring her back.'

'Yes, but by talking to her friend, has it occurred to you that while Anya wants to see you because she thinks it would be helpful to you, you in turn could do something to help Anya? Listening to her story might help her, she was after all your sister's best friend.'

Before Miles could answer, Keith's phone began rumbling in his jacket pocket. 'You're not allowed mobile phones in here, Chief Inspector,' Miles said.

Keith ignored him and walked over to the window. 'Yes Jack,' he said. He listened intently and while he did so Miles watched him. Keith Penrose was not a tall man but there was a strength about him. He was broad-shouldered, stocky even but he had an energy which belied his years – Miles knew him to be nearer sixty than fifty. He had a shock of dark hair peppered with grey which showed no signs of thinning and while it was cut as short as was appropriate for a policeman, there was a wildness about it. He was good-looking in a unconventional way, with a slightly crooked nose – presumably the result of some long ago rugby game – and a firm square chin. His eyes were bright blue, intelligent, enquiring but at the same time compassionate. He is the kind of man I would have liked for a father, Miles thought, and look what I got instead.

Keith ended the call abruptly and turned back to Miles. 'What are you staring at?' he asked.

'Nothing,' Miles said. 'What's up?'

'Police business,' Keith said firmly.

'Oh, come on, I'm stuck here with nothing to do all day.'

'A body,' said Keith, 'over in St Erth, well a skeleton actually. I'm required on the scene, though God knows why, it's nearly dark, I won't be able to see anything.'

Miles smiled at him. 'So you began your day with a visit from a beautiful girl and it ends with a skeleton in St Erth. I think your day is deteriorating, Chief Inspector.'

Keith studied him in silence for a moment. 'You could make it right, young man. If you would just agree to see Anya, my day would end magnificently. I do truly believe a meeting would do you both good.'

Miles hesitated for a moment. 'OK, I'll do it,' he said, 'but only for you not for me, I don't think it's going to help me at all.'

Keith let out a sigh. 'Thanks for that. I'll get her to ring you here.' He glanced briefly at the phone by Miles's bed, and then hurried to the door.

There he paused, turning back to smile at Miles. 'Now don't you go running off anywhere, will you?'

'Fat chance of that, Chief Inspector. Hey, you didn't bring me any grapes.'

'I'll bring you a truckload of grapes,' said Keith firmly, 'if you're kind to Anya.'

3

Miles had been right, his day had definitely deteriorated, Keith thought, as he pulled into the drive of his home and glanced at his watch. It was past eight; Barbara was not going to be amused. The day that had begun so promisingly with Anya's visit and then seeing Felicity again had ended in an hastily-erected tent over a muddy vegetable patch in the back garden of a cottage in St Erth. There had been an hysterical woman to calm down who had been innocently turning over the soil for the winter, prior to mulching it, she explained. Instead of digging up the long-lost potatoes she had found herself staring at a skull. There was a morose husband who kept telling her to pipe down and two school-age children obviously taking a profound, if ghoulish, interest in proceedings. There was little they could do tonight. His sergeant, Jack Curnow, was going to check out the previous occupants of the house and then they would have to wait for the initial forensic report giving some indication of the age and sex of the skeleton. He would go back to the house in the morning to interview the occupants properly when everybody had calmed down.

For some reason he felt extremely tired as he levered himself out of the car. Maybe seeing Felicity again had taken it toll, while Anya and Miles had created their own emotional demands. It had been a wearying day; he just hoped Barbara was in a reasonable mood. He let himself quietly in through the kitchen door and to his surprise he saw Barbara sitting at the kitchen table with a glass of wine. With a sinking heart, he saw there were no obvious signs of supper preparation.

She glanced up as he came into the room. 'Hello Keith,' she said listlessly. No recriminations: something wasn't right. He put down his briefcase and walked across the room giving her a perfunctory kiss on the top of the head.

'I think I'll join you in one of those,' he said. He reached for a glass out of the kitchen cabinet and it was only as he turned round that he saw the bleak expression on his wife's face. 'What's happened?' he said, in sudden alarm, fear clutching at him. 'The children, are they alright?'

Barbara glanced up at him. 'The children are fine, as far as I know.'

Relief flooded through him. Ever since his daughter Carly had been diagnosed with Hodgkin's Lymphoma, Keith had been plagued with irrational fears, even though she appeared to have made a full recovery. He reached for the bottle and poured himself a glass of red wine, sitting down heavily with his wife at the kitchen table.

'So what's up then?' he asked.

'I've been made redundant, Keith, after all these years.'

'Bloody hell! I'm so sorry,' said Keith. He reached out his hand and covered hers which lay on the kitchen table. He squeezed it; there was no response. 'Why, why you?' Keith asked.

Barbara let out a sigh. 'Because I'm old, I suppose. They're doing some radical streamlining because of a shortage of funding, of course. They just don't need so many people, I knew it was coming. I don't know why it is such a shock, I just wasn't expecting it to be so soon.'

'When are you leaving?' Keith asked.

'I've left,' said Barbara, 'I cleared my desk this afternoon.'

'Poor you,' said Keith. He was well aware of how much Barbara's job meant to her. That must have been awful.'

'It's compulsory redundancy.' Barbara said. 'I could have stayed on for another three months but

34

I felt that would be humiliating. Once I knew they didn't want me any more, I just wanted to go as quickly as possible.'

'Quite right too,' said Keith, his stomach rumbling audibly. 'Look, you obviously haven't done anything about supper, and I'm not surprised. Why don't we go out for dinner and cheer ourselves up?'

Barbara shook her head. 'I couldn't face it. Maybe you could make one of your Spanish omelettes.'

Keith's heart sank. He had missed lunch completely and there had only been a hurried piece of toast at breakfast. He was starving.

'OK, I'll do that.' Keith stood up and began rummaging in the fridge assembling what he would need for the omelette. 'So what are you going to do?' he asked. 'You don't need another job, we'll be fine financially.'

'Yes, we will,' Barbara agreed, 'the redundancy package is usually very generous. I've been there so long I don't know how they can afford to make me redundant really.'

'So what are you going to do?' Keith repeated as he began cracking eggs into a bowl.

'I thought I might go and see Carly,' Barbara said.

'In Australia?' Keith paused in his

preparations, staring at Barbara in amazement.

'Of course in Australia,' said Barbara, 'that's where she is, isn't she?'

'When?' Keith asked.

'Well, now, I thought,' said Barbara. 'I was hoping you might come too.'

'I can't possibly go now,' Keith said, 'we're just starting a potential new murder enquiry and I have a lot of loose ends to tie up.'

'Why does that not surprise me?' Barbara said, bitterly. 'You can never go away in the summer because you say that's your busiest time and you can never go away in the winter because you're always tying up loose ends.' She gave Keith a sly look. 'Carly will be so disappointed if she has to put up with just me. You know she's a daddy's girl.'

Keith did not rise to the bait.

'I can't go at the moment, Barbara, and are you sure you want to right now? It seems quite an extreme reaction, you must still be in shock.'

'I think I deserve it, Keith,' she said. 'I've worked very hard for all these years, looked after you, raised the children, mostly single-handed, and now I've been made redundant but at least they are giving me a nice sum of money. I'm owed this holiday with or without you – it'll soon be summer in Australia, you know.'

'So when will you go?' Keith asked.

'As soon as possible,' said Barbara, firmly. 'When we've had supper I'll look online and see what flights I can get.'

'Have you discussed it with Carly?'

'No, not yet,' said Barbara, 'I've only just decided.'

'She may not have room for you to stay,' Keith said, 'it's only a small flat they're living in.'

'In which case I'll stay at a hotel nearby,' said Barbara. 'I'm going to do this Keith, and frankly, I don't need your blessing.'

'Of course you have my blessing,' said Keith, tiredly, returning to the chopping board and dicing an onion with concentrated ferocity.

'If you're not going to come yourself,' Barbara continued, 'at least you could behave like you're pleased for me.'

'I am pleased for you,' said Keith, 'I'm just surprised, that's all. When will you be back?'

'I'll be back in time for Christmas, I won't leave you on your own for that.'

'Is Will staying in Germany for Christmas?'

Barbara nodded. 'Yes, I think there might be a girl out there. He hasn't said so but he was very adamant about staying over the holiday period. There must be a reason, I reckon it's a girl.'

'Good, I'm glad,' said Keith, 'but you don't have to worry about me at Christmas, I can always go up to my sister. Betty and Ed would be prepared to put up with me, I'm sure of that and I'm on duty over New Year in any event.'

'No change there then,' said Barbara.

'Look, don't let's argue,' said Keith. He turned from the stove to face his wife. 'I'm really sorry about your redundancy and I think it is a good idea, you going to Australia, I agree you deserve a break. I'm sorry I can't come with you and all I'm saying is, don't rush back on my account, I'll be fine.'

'You don't really need anybody, do you, Keith,' Barbara said.

'That's not fair,' Keith bit back, 'I'm just trying to make things easy for you.'

'Easy for yourself more like,' said Barbara, 'I expect you'll be glad to see the back of me.'

Keith did not trust himself to speak. He continued chopping and whisking and a few minutes later delivered two plates of fluffy omelette on to the table.

'I said I wasn't hungry,' said Barbara.

'Suit yourself,' said Keith, his patience exhausted. He poured them both another glass of wine and attacked his omelette. When he had finished, he swapped plates with Barbara and ate hers as well. Still in silence he cleared the plates away and put them in the dishwasher. 'Would you like some coffee?'

'No thanks,' she said, 'I'm going to look up some flights.'

'OK.' Keith made himself a coffee, he was dog-tired but too restless for television. He took his coffee upstairs to the bedroom, stripped off his clothes and had a hot shower. It was only 9 o'clock but he looked longingly at the bed and decided it was the best place for him. He climbed between the sheets and turned out the bedside light, a drowsiness already creeping over him. As he slipped into a deep sleep his last conscious thought was not of his wife and her impending trip to Australia, not of Miles and his sister, not of the skeleton in St Erth nor even of his beloved daughter Carly. His last conscious thought was of Felicity Paradise's bright smile, bright enough even to eclipse her mad multi-coloured sweater.

Dr Horace Greenaway and Chief Inspector Keith Penrose went way back. They had first met as grubby little boys at the infants' school in Ladock, but while they had quite liked each other, they had very little in common. At an early age Keith had shown a great interest and aptitude for sport whereas Horace, a slightly podgy little boy, preferred to have his head in a book. They had drifted apart because they had not enough in common to form a lasting friendship. However they were bright boys, bright and ambitious, and both had won scholarships to study 'A' Levels at Truro School which is where they re-established their relationship and cemented a friendship which would last a lifetime. They had sunk their first pint together, ogled girls together, studied late into the night together – then their paths had parted once more. Keith had joined the police force initially at the Met and Horace had gone up to Cambridge to read medicine and then to specialise in forensic science; he had not returned to Cornwall for many years. Keith, by contrast, a committed Cornishman, was back home as soon as his training was complete. When Horace, too, finally returned home, both men were delighted to be working together again, even if their relentless banter bewildered their colleagues.

'What have you got for me, Horace?' Keith bellowed down the phone.

'It's eight-forty-five,' Horace responded, 'I haven't had the chap with me for more than ten minutes, what on earth do you expect?'

'A young chap, is he?' Keith asked.

'Stop fishing, Penrose, he's not old, he's not young; in his late forties or early fifties I would think. I'll know a lot more later if you'll just get off the phone and let me get on with my job.'

'But surely you can tell me more or less how

long he's been dead?' Keith persisted.

'I can't,' said Horace, 'and I'm not even going to try. You've provided me with a skeleton so obviously the man has been dead for some years, but it's a boggy piece of ground where you found him, decomposition could have happened quite quickly. Anyway, what's up? You don't sound your normal cheerful self.'

'Sorry,' said Keith, 'I had a bit of a domestic last night.'

'I'm not surprised,' said Horace, 'how that poor woman puts up with you I do not know.'

In fact there was no love lost between Barbara and Horace. Horace considered Barbara dull and not good enough for Keith. Barbara considered Horace to be a flamboyant idiot and much too pleased with himself.

'Barbara's just lost her job,' Keith said.

'She must have been coming up for retirement anyway, surely?'

'Not for another four or five years,' said Keith.

'Pension, redundancy, that sort of thing?' Horace queried.

'Oh yes, financially there shouldn't be a problem but it's not so good to be suddenly chucked on the scrapheap.'

'It will happen to us any moment,' Horace said, gloomily.

'You're right,' said Keith, 'but they're bound to scrap you ahead of me, I'm a far greater asset.'

'That's better, both rude and misguided,' said Horace, 'you had me worried there for a moment. What is she going to do, Barbara that is?'

'Go to Australia,' said Keith.

'Good Lord, is she leaving you for another man?'

'She is going to see Carly, at least that's what she's telling me,' said Keith.

'Well, good luck to her. You don't mind her going, do you?'

'No, no, of course not,' said Keith, 'I think it's a good idea. It's just that I'm supposed to be going too and of course I can't, work comes first.'

'This skeleton could wait, he's waited long enough.'

'How long would that be exactly?' Keith asked.

'Sod off, Chief Inspector, you're really starting to annoy me.'

The atmosphere was a lot less volatile at Tanner's Cottage in St Erth when Keith and his sergeant arrived. Both Jenny and Desmond Gilbertson had taken the day off work. The scene of crime team was already established in the garden. Jenny made everyone a cup of coffee and they settled down in the Gilbertsons' sitting room with a fine view of the forensic team hard at work.

'I just don't know how I'm going to be able to go on living here?' Jenny said, staring out of the window.

'Don't be ridiculous,' her husband responded, 'that body's been down there all these years and it hasn't bothered us, and now it's gone.'

'It's all very well for you, Des. When I dug up that, that head and saw it staring at me, I thought I was going to die of shock.'

'So you've said, several times,' said her husband, unsympathetically.

'Look,' said Keith, 'I appreciate this is a big shock for everyone and it's hardly pleasant to have your garden so thoroughly,' he glanced towards the window searching for a word, 'so thoroughly investigated.'

'Destroyed more like,' said Des, morosely.

'How long have you lived here?' Jack asked, his notebook at the ready.

'Nearly ten years,' said Desmond.

'And before that?'

'We rented a little flat in Hayle,' said Jenny, 'that's where we lived when we first got married. I wish we still did.'

'Don't be ridiculous,' said Des. 'Where would we have put the kids? We bought this place because we had to and the mortgage is going to take us the rest of our lives to pay off.'

'Who lived here before?' Keith asked.

'I knew you'd ask that,' Jenny said, 'but our deeds are with our solicitors. I'm just trying to remember her name. A lovely lady, she was a widow, the cottage had got too big for her to manage.'

'Where did she go?' Keith asked.

'St Ives, I think. I wish I could remember her name.'

'Don't worry,' said Keith, 'my sergeant is on to it.'

Jack nodded.

Keith turned his attention to Desmond. 'So I suppose I'm right in saying you have no idea who the body is?'

Desmond stared aggressively at Keith for a moment. 'No, I bloody well don't and neither does Jenny. You saw the state of it, it's been down there for years, long before we bought this cottage.'

'Maybe, maybe not,' said Keith, 'we're waiting for forensics to tell us, but I understand the nature of the soil is such that decomposition could have happened quite quickly. Ten years is quite long enough to reduce a body to a skeleton.'

'What are you suggesting?' Desmond said.

'I'm suggesting nothing,' said Keith mildly, 'I'm simply asking you the question. Have you any idea as to the identity of the body?'

'No, he hasn't,' Jenny butted in. 'I thought you had come here to be sympathetic, not start accusing us of things. Do we look like the sort of people who would bury a body in our garden?'

Keith sighed; he was not in the mood for this. 'You'd be surprised how ordinary-looking the most vicious of villains can appear.' He regretted the words as soon as he had spoken them.

Desmond jumped to his feet. 'I think I'd better call my solicitor if you're going to start making accusations.'

Keith stood up too. 'No, no, look I'm sorry, I'm simply saying that until the body has been carbon-dated we don't know what we're looking for and I have to ask you the question as a matter of routine. I apologise if I've upset you both.' He included Jenny in a tentative smile.

Desmond remained standing. 'Is there anything else then?' he asked belligerently.

'No, no, that's all for now,' said Keith. 'Come on Jack.'

Once outside the cottage Keith let out a sigh. 'I handled that well, didn't I?' he said.

'You have been a little more tactful in your time, sir,' Jack said, with a grin. 'Mind you it was quite tempting to wind up that Des character –

what a plonker!'

'Still,' said Keith, 'no excuse for upsetting the public. Do we know who lived there before?'

'Yes, Violet Symonds. She and her husband, David, bought Tanner's Cottage in 1961 and they just had one child, a son, Andrew. Gossip has it that David ran off with another woman and Violet sold the house some years later. She has a ground floor flat in St Ives now, in Bedford Road, bottom end near the shops, she must be in her seventies I would imagine,' said Jack. 'Would you like me to go and see her?'

'No, I'll do that,' said Keith, hastily.

'You won't go upsetting some nice little old lady, will you sir?'

'I shall ignore that,' said Keith. 'You go back to the station and start looking up missing persons' data in the area, going back twenty to thirty years and I suppose you had better find out who lived in the house before the Symonds. We need a date – if bloody Horace would just pull his finger out – could you chase him up?'

'I'll try, sir,' said Jack, 'but he normally responds better to your bullying than mine.'

'Go,' ordered Keith.

Fifteen minutes later he was parked in Bedford Road outside Violet Symonds's flat. He sat quietly in the car for a moment or two collecting his thoughts, trying not to think that he was only a few minutes' walk from Felicity's cottage. He had wanted to see Violet Symonds in person anyway, but the opportunity to come to St Ives could not be resisted. Now he was here though, he knew he should not break the unwritten rule they had set themselves. There was no justification for seeing Felicity two days running, unless of course he could convince himself that she needed to know the outcome of his meeting with Miles.

Violet Symonds looked like everyone's ideal grandmother. She was small and round with wispy snow-white hair pulled up into a little bun. She wore half-moon glasses on the end of her nose and behind those a pair of kind, grey eyes studied Keith as he made his introduction.

'Come in,' she said, 'the flat is a bit of a mess, I wasn't expecting visitors.' The flat was bright and airy with high ceilings. Violet led Keith through to her kitchen at the back and put the kettle on. 'Take a seat, dear,' she said, indicating to the table.

Keith studied Violet as she busied herself with the teapot. He was not used to such acceptance. Normally the police turning up on someone's doorstep unannounced caused a fair degree of nervousness, apprehension, panic even, but he might have been the local plumber come to fix her drains for all the concern or interest Violet was showing in his reason for visiting her. But when she turned to him to ask, 'Sugar, milk?' he could see there was nothing much wrong with Violet Symonds. She was bright as a button.

At last the preparations for tea and biscuits were complete, the tea poured into some fine bone china and Violet lowered herself gingerly into a chair opposite Keith. 'Now dear,' she said, 'what can I do for you?'

'I've come from your former home, Tanner's Cottage in St Erth,' Keith said, and paused for a moment while she absorbed this. 'I'm afraid, Mrs Symonds, you need to prepare yourself for something of a shock.'

'Get on with it, please,' she said.

'We've found a body, well a skeleton, in the back garden. The people to whom you sold the house, the Gilbertsons, they found it or rather Jenny, Mrs Gilbertson did when she was digging over her vegetable patch.'

'That must have been a terrible shock for her,' Violet said.

Keith studied her; she had paled slightly but otherwise seemed unaffected by the news. 'Yes it was,' he admitted, 'she was pretty hysterical last night, and no wonder. I suppose it's a stupid question, Mrs Symonds, but you've no idea how a body could have ended up in your former back garden?'

'No idea at all,' Violet confirmed. 'How long has it been there?'

'We don't know yet. You lived at the property a long time, didn't you?'

Violet nodded. 'Most of my adult life really, my husband and I moved in the early sixties, 1962 I think, and I sold up about ten years ago.'

'So I understand,' said Keith. 'Why did you leave?'

'It all got too much for me, the cottage, I mean. I know it's only a small place but it's too big for one person and the garden and everything, I'm in my seventies now and this flat suits me very well. I just have to walk a few yards to the Co-op and the chemist, it's all so handy.'

Keith smiled at her. 'Yes, I can see that.'

'I should have moved sooner but I was attached to the old place, having been there so long.'

'Has your husband died?' Keith asked, thinking it the most tactful way to broach the subject.

'My husband ran off and left me.'

'Oh, I'm so sorry,' said Keith.

'No need to be, dear,' said Violet. 'It happened years ago, he met someone younger, prettier, the usual story and they took off to Australia. He died out there, about ten years back from cancer, I believe.'

'And children?' Keith asked.

'Just one, a son, Andy. He's died too I'm afraid.' This time there was a genuine expression of pain across her face. 'It was Christmas 1983, he was a bit of a wild one, his motorbike hit a patch of black ice, mercifully he died immediately. The policeman at the time told me there would have been no pain, I hope he was right.'

'I'm sure he was,' Keith said, 'we don't say things like that unless they are true.'

Violet nodded and there was a silence between them. 'More tea, Chief Inspector?'

Keith shook his head. 'No, thanks. So can I take it that you had no idea there was a body in your garden?'

'None whatsoever,' Violet replied.

'And you have no idea who it could be?'

'No,' said Violet.

'Were you much of a gardener?' Keith asked.

'Not much,' said Violet, 'I liked to keep the garden neat and tidy. David, my husband, did have a vegetable patch out back but after he'd gone, I let it grow over. I had a son to raise and a job to hold down to support us, I hadn't got time to mess around growing vegetables.'

'So there is really nothing you can think of which might help us.'

'I'm afraid not, said Violet, smiling at him over the top of her glasses.

'We'll know more soon,' said Keith, 'the age of the victim and how long they've been in the ground. I'll keep you informed obviously.'

'Thank you, dear.'

Keith stood up and began to walk towards the front door, turning as he reached it. 'You didn't seem surprised to see me?' Keith said.

Violet studied him quizzically for a moment. 'You mean I wasn't worried that you were a policeman?'

'Something like that,' Keith said, smiling at her.

'I've had a few bad experiences in my life. Nothing that can happen to me at my ripe old age can be that bad.'

'I'm sorry,' said Keith, wondering what on earth she meant.

'No need to be, I'm quite alright, I'm used to it now, taking life as it comes.'

Felicity was sitting in the weak winter sun on her balcony, wrapped in a coat and talking animatedly on the phone making Christmas plans. She had just established that her god-daughter Ellie would not be coming to Cornwall for Christmas but would be spending it with her father, Josh, but that her son, James and family, would be coming. 'How are we going to fit everyone in?' Felicity wailed at her daughter Mel, who lived a few miles away in Hayle in an ugly but marvellously-positioned house on the edge of the estuary.

'Stop fussing Mum, it will be fine, everyone can bunk down here. The children can all share, which they'll love and James and Trish can go in Charlie's room. We'll just have to come up with some temporary double bed for them.'

'Well, let me do that,' said Felicity, 'what about buying a futon or something and that could be useful in Charlie's room long term?'

'Fine,' said Mel, 'that or a sofa bed, we can have a look around and see what we can find.'

'Good,' said Felicity, 'we have a plan.'

There was a slight bleakness in Felicity's voice which her daughter picked up. 'That means you'll be all alone in your house, Mum. Obviously you'll come over each day but it's not the same as staying here is it? I suppose there is always the sofa.'

'Don't be silly,' said Felicity, 'I'll be fine.'

'Alternatively,' said Mel, laughing, 'Martin and I could come and stay in your house and you could come and stay here, that would be very restful.'

'Thanks, but no thanks,' said Felicity. 'I adore

my grandchildren but there are limits.'

They began chatting about arrangements over the next few days. 'Do you need any babysitting done this weekend,' Felicity asked, 'only I've got a stack of work and I just need to plan when I'm going to do it.'

'No, we're fine this weekend, Mum, thanks.'

'OK then, so I'll see you on...' A familiar figure was walking up the street towards her. Felicity stood up, phone still to her ear and peered over the top of the balcony. There was no mistaking him.

'Mum, are you there?' Mel asked.

'Yes, yes, sorry darling, I'll see you on Thursday.'

'Great. I need to be into work really early.'

'I'll be there at seven o'clock sharp, I promise. Bye darling.' She turned off her phone and peered over the balcony, staring down at the man who stood below her. 'What are you doing here?' she asked.

'I had a visit to make in Bedford Road so I just thought I'd come by on the off-chance you were in and bring you up to date on Miles.'

'You'd better come up,' she said.

'I was thinking,' Keith replied, 'it's such a beautiful day, why don't you join me for a walk along the Wharf.'

'I'll be right down,' she called back. He was

53

quite right, she thought as she busied herself shutting the French windows, finding Harvey's lead and a pair of gloves, the intimacy of her home was not a good place for them to be.

Harvey catapulted through the door to where Keith was waiting, dragging Felicity behind him. 'Hello Harvey,' Keith said, bending down to pat the little dog. He straightened up and smiled at Felicity. 'See what I mean,' he said gesturing around him, 'what a wonderful day.'

'I know,' Felicity smiled back. 'Come on, let's go.'

'I can't be long,' said Keith, 'I've got a skeleton to identify in St Erth.'

Felicity grinned at him. 'You do have a fun life.'

'It's an odd one though,' said Keith, 'I don't know how long it's been there, I'm no pathologist, heaven knows. '

'A skeleton,' said Felicity, 'you do have all the luck.'

'Stop the cheek, right there,' said Keith firmly, 'just remember I'm a very important person with a very important job to do.'

'Yes, Chief Inspector,' said Felicity, meekly.

'Right, now let me tell you about Miles.'

The young man in question was sitting up in his

hospital bed wondering if he had died and gone to Heaven. The girl sitting on the chair beside him was quite beautiful, the same dark colouring as his own, with long shiny brown hair, and beautiful almond-shaped eyes. He wished he had shaved better that morning, he wished he had put on clean pyjamas, and brushed his hair but she had rung from the hospital lobby to ask if she could see him and that was all of three minutes ago. He'd had no time to prepare himself in any way, particularly not emotionally. They had shaken hands formally and now Anya was sitting on the visitor's chair where Keith Penrose had been the day before.

'I was in Truro,' she explained, 'and suddenly I thought if I don't do it now, come and see you now, I might not be brave enough, I might leave it a week or two and then you'd be back in London and I'd have missed the chance. So I plucked up the courage and here I am.'

'Why did you need courage?' Miles asked.

'The inspector said it was OK to ring you but I wasn't sure you really wanted to see me, I thought maybe he had talked you into it.'

Miles decided there was no point in doing anything other than speaking the truth. 'The fact is,' he said, 'I want to know more about my sister, of course I do, but I don't want to hear the details of her life.' He searched Anya's face looking for understanding. 'That's really cowardly, isn't it?'

'No,' Anya replied, 'not only is it not cowardly, but actually I don't want to talk about the details of our life either. I've moved on, I've put all that behind me, I've put it in a drawer and locked it away. It is the only way I stand a chance of having a normal life.'

'I'm sorry,' Miles said, humbly, 'how selfish of me, I was only seeing this from my point of view, not from yours.'

She reached out and put her hand gently on his arm. 'It's OK. Let me tell you about your sister.' Miles nodded, he was suddenly choked and unable to speak. 'You look very like her. Despite the life we led she was full of fun and laughter. She was a wonderful friend to me, kind, motherly, she took care of me. I was so lucky. When I ran away from the orphanage I was only fourteen and she found me on a street corner, bad things had happened to me.' Anya's face clouded. 'She took me back to her room, she cared for me.' There was a silence between them. 'Her obsession in life was to find you,' Anya continued, 'she told me about you within, what, half an hour of us meeting. She had found the name of your parents, she had checked out the adoption records but she didn't know your new name. You know you were called Nicholae?'

Miles nodded. 'I do now.'

'Then your father went missing in St Ives and it was all over the papers. She spotted an old English newspaper one day and it showed a picture of the family, you, your mother and your father, she recognised you at once – well, how could she not, you were so very alike. So she knew your name was Miles now, and from that moment on she was determined to come to England. However, when she found someone willing to give her a job over here, she refused to go unless I could come too.'

Miles let out a great sigh. 'It was a bad decision though, wasn't it? The man who offered you a job was the man who killed her, her murderer.'

'Yes, but she wasn't to know that. Our life in England was bad, but it was worth it. From Marianna's point of view she was in the same country as you, she just had to find you.'

'And the stupid thing is,' said Miles, 'she went all the way to Cornwall when, like you, I was mostly living in London.'

'But she did find you,' Anya said, 'she did achieve what she set out to do.'

'And the moment she finds me I run away because I can't take what she has to tell me.'

'What did she tell you?' Anya asked gently.

'She told me that I was adopted, I had no idea.'

'You didn't know?' Anya was amazed.

'No, my parents had kept it from me. To start

with when Marianna was telling me that she was my sister and that we had shared a cot together in the orphanage, I just couldn't believe it, there was just so much to take in. I started by thinking she was mad and then I began to realise that she was telling the truth and I could see the likeness between us, and it was all too much, I couldn't handle it, I couldn't believe my parents had lied to me all those years. I just ran away, left the house, ran down onto the beach...' he paused, 'and then when I came back, she was dead.' He began to sob, great racking sobs that shook his narrow frame. Without hesitation Anya stood up and moved to his side; she put her arms around him and drew his head onto her breast, stroking his hair as if he was a small child. It was several minutes before Miles could control himself but at last he drew away searching on his bedside table for some tissue. 'I'm so sorry,' he said, 'I don't know what you must think of me.'

'It's OK,' said Anya, 'have you... have you?'

'Have I cried like this before? No,' he said.

'I thought not.' She retreated to the chair and sat down.

'There are so many "if onlys",' Miles said, blowing his nose and wiping his eyes. 'I go over and over and over it in my head and it never comes out right.'

'Marianna loved you, she loved you dearly as a baby and she would have loved you now as the man you have become. If you waste one day, one hour, one minute being sad about what happened then you are doing her a disservice. Above everything else she would have wanted you to be happy, to love life, to take the opportunities given to you, to live for both of you. Thinking what might have been is pointless, what's past is past. You can't change it, but you can live the kind of life she would have wanted for you...' Anya paused. 'Sorry, I didn't mean to lecture.'

Miles was staring at her. 'Anya?'

'Yes,' she said.

'Will you come and see me again?'

4

'Keith, it's Horace.'

'About bloody time,' Keith said. 'What have you been doing?'

'My job,' said Horace, 'as always – carefully, precisely so I make sure that I give the Constabulary the right information.'

'OK,' said Keith, 'just get on with it would you.'

'Male, late forties or maybe early fifties, five foot eleven – a manual labourer I would think, seems to have been a strong chap.'

'How long has he been in the ground?' Keith asked.

In my view only snce the late seventies, 1978, 1979, not longer.'

'How did he die?' Keith asked.

'He has a fractured skull, but not a very severe injury. At first I thought it could have been caused by the woman's spade when she dug him up but it wasn't, it was a definite fracture but certainly it wouldn't have killed him. It would have given him a nasty headache, maybe even rendered him unconscious for a while – a few minutes I would have thought but no more.'

'So do we know how he died?' Keith asked.

'The bullet rattling around in his ribcage was a bit of a give-away,' said Horace.

Jack Curnow was waiting for Keith back at the Station.

'Any luck with the Gilbertsons' neighbours?' Jack had been engaged in house-to-house enquiries immediately around Tanner's Cottage. He shook his head.

'There's not a single neighbour who's lived in the area for more than five years.'

'It's a sign of the times, boy,' Keith said, smiling at his sergeant. 'We're lucky you know, a couple of Cornish lads who've never really strayed far from our roots – so many people are dotted around the country, around the world come to that, never staying long enough to call any place home.'

'Are you thinking about Carly?' Jack asked.

'I wasn't,' Keith said, 'but now you come to mention it…' His voice trailed off.

'She'll come home, sir,' Jack said. 'Most people do after a few years of adventure.'

'Why would she?' Keith asked. 'She's having a

wonderful life out there; they've both got good jobs, what on earth has this damp, overcrowded little island got to offer her?'

'Family, friends and it's her home,' Jack said, firmly.

'Well, it will be interesting to see what Barbara makes of her life out there.'

'Mrs Penrose is going to Australia?'

'For a holiday,' said Keith 'She's been made redundant and she needs a break so she is going out to see Carly. Her flight leaves next week, next Tuesday. I was going to ask you to cover for me, I'm going to take her up to Heathrow.'

'Yes, of course,' said Jack and something in his boss's face made it clear that the subject was now closed.

'I've had the report from Horace,' Keith said, 'a verbal one anyway. The victim was male, used to doing manual work, and has been in the ground since the late seventies which puts his demise firmly in the frame of when the Symonds lived there.'

'What did you think of Mrs Symonds?'

'A sweet old lady,' said Keith, 'charming, offered me a lovely cup of tea. She is lonely too, her husband ran off with some floozy to Australia and her son died in a motorcycle accident.'

'Died, are you sure?' Jack frowned and leafed through some papers he was holding in his hand.

'Andrew, the name is Andrew, her son, that is?'

'Yes, that's right,' said Keith.

'There is no record of his death.'

'Maybe you just missed it,' said Keith.

'Maybe,' Jack agreed reluctantly.

'Though,' Keith admitted, 'it's unlikely, knowing you and your paperwork.'

Jack grinned at his boss. 'Well sir, it's having such a wonderful role model, I try daily to be as efficient as you.'

They smiled at one another and Keith raised a mock fist. 'Get out of here.'

'I'll check out the son, sir, and shall I widen the house-to-house?'

'No,' said Keith, 'I've just got a feeling we may have struck gold with this allegedly dead son. Come back to me on him as soon as you can, before we spend any more taxpayers' money.'

'Will do, sir.'

Keith sat down heavily at his desk and surveyed the files which almost obscured it. He swore they bred overnight. He would make a start on them right now, he thought, while he was waiting for Jack to report back. He wanted to get away in good time this evening because finally he had persuaded Barbara to let him take her out to dinner. There had been all sorts of excuses for some reason – her packing, spring-cleaning the house, batch-cooking for the freezer.

'Please don't cook anything for me,' Keith had said. 'I'll simply go to the pub.'

'That's what I'm afraid of, all those chips,' Barbara had said, sharply. She was still angry with him for not coming to Australia with her, but the fact was he really didn't want to go, though why he wasn't quite sure.

Felicity Paradise was in high spirits. Six weeks ago she had taken two of her paintings to the little Windward Gallery in Penzance. Much to her astonishment they had sold within a few days and she had replaced them. Now they had asked for six. She was astonished but delighted and the gallery owner, Thomas Ward, and his assistant Sarah were thrilled with Felicity's success. She had started painting in a new style almost by chance. She had been illustrating a children's book and had painted some rather wacky scenes of St Ives involving the hectic use of primary colours. The publisher had loved them and had said maybe she should try developing the style into a few pictures to sell to visitors and this was the result. If she could sell this many paintings out of season, just think what she could do in the summer; it could revolutionise her finances which were always somewhat precarious.

'We'll be rich and famous yet,' she said to Harvey. Harvey was curled up asleep on the back seat and seemed unimpressed. Felicity was concentrating hard – she was driving home on the back road from Penzance, it was dark and foggy and she drove slowly and carefully down into Nancledra. As she came out of the village on the other side, up on to the moor, the mist swirled around, looking both beautiful and sinister, lit by an almost full moon that now and again made its appearance from behind the troubled clouds. 'I'm happy,' she thought to herself and wondered when that had last been the case.

Her husband Charlie had been dead now for over seven years and for much of that time, she felt she had been going through the motions, smiling outwardly but dead inside. So much had happened. The highlight of course had been the very successful and happy marriage of her daughter, Mel, and as a result two wonderful grandchildren living on her doorstep. But against that was the death of her best friend Gilla, which had left a huge gap in her life and the unsettling knowledge that Charlie had not been all he seemed, that he had carried secrets she knew nothing about until after his death. There had been the move from Oxford to St Ives. Her Oxford friends had thought she was mad but she had no regrets, particularly now Mel had chosen to live in Cornwall too. It had all taken a great deal of adjustment and, if she was being kind to herself, a certain degree of courage too.

Threading through it all, of course, was her relationship with Keith Penrose. They had stepped back from the precipice of having an affair, knowing it would have suited neither of them, but she loved him and knew he loved her and that knowledge gave her strength. Despite the fact that nothing could ever come of their relationship, she knew that he would always be there for her, and that was what counted. Now this unexpected success, this escalation in her career, had given her a whole new dimension – suddenly there was a point to the future which she realised had been lacking before. As a wife and a mother, both roles she had relished, she had always played second fiddle, first to her husband's career and then to her children's lives, taking jobs in local schools, teaching art because that fitted around everyone else. Now she could do anything. The sense of freedom was exhilarating and she wondered why it had taken her so long to reach this point.

She parked up in her usual spot in Barnoon car park; the sea below was inky black, there was no sign of the moon now. She clipped the lead on a reluctant Harvey and began picking her way through the narrow streets towards home. Even before she reached her front door, she sensed there was something wrong. Harvey did too. He was always anxious to get home and was pulling on the lead as normal, when suddenly he stopped and backed away, close to her legs, at precisely the same moment that she felt her own sense of unease.

'Come on, Harvey,' she said, stoically. They walked cautiously down the street. Her wonderful purple front door was hanging at an odd angle, splintered from the lock. Felicity gasped. She glanced nervously over her shoulder and looked up and down the street but there was no one about on this cold dank night. She looked up at her balcony; the French windows were shut, there was no light inside her house. She hesitated. Should she call the police first or should she go inside and see the damage? With only a moment's hesitation, she squeezed round the half-opened door and turned on the hall light. 'Is anyone there?' she called out. The silence that followed was reassuring – instinctively she knew she was alone. She glanced down at her little dog; he too seemed to have relaxed a little. She unclipped his lead. 'Let's go and take a look,' she said, her voice trembling slightly.

She climbed the stairs to her kitchen, switching on lights as she went, listening intently for a footstep or the sound of any kind of movement. There was none. She reached the kitchen and looked around – it was just as she had left it, nothing was touched or disturbed. She put her bag on the kitchen table and Harvey walked over to his basket by the Aga and collapsed into it. 'Well, you're certainly not worried, are you?' Felicity said.

One hurdle remained. She advanced towards the half-open door to her little sitting room which adjoined the kitchen. The darkness she could see through the door felt menacing yet Harvey seemed relaxed, no one could still be inside... Suddenly she knew what had happened. She turned on the light and looked over towards her mantelpiece. There it was, a bare piece of wall with just the dark outline of where a small picture had hung. 'Oh no,' she cried. She glanced wildly around the room, which was otherwise undisturbed. She ran back downstairs and looked in both bedrooms, her own and the spare room: no one had been near them. Someone had broken into her home and taken the one thing of true value she had. It was an early Constable, which had belonged to Charlie's mother, the one relic the poor woman had been allowed to keep from her family home which had been sold off to meet debts. Charlie had called the painting 'The Insurance'. He and his mother had lived alone in genteel poverty but they had never been tempted to sell the painting. It was his mother's heritage, then his and now it had passed to Felicity. She had every intention in passing it on to her son James – and now it had gone.

She trudged upstairs and into the sitting room again to stare at the blank wall, as if to convince herself that it was really missing. It was insured of course, but that was not the point. It was a true family heirloom and it also stood for something. Despite the hardship which Charlie and his mother had endured, a hardship which could have been entirely removed by the selling of the painting, they had chosen not to do so, chosen to hang onto it for its beauty and for what the painting stood for, a lost way of life… and now it was gone.

Hot tears began running down her face. How could she have been so stupid, why hadn't she fitted an alarm system? It had never occurred to her that she needed one; she often went out and left the front door entirely unlocked. The desire to ring Keith Penrose was almost overwhelming but instead she groped blindly around in her bag until she found her mobile and then began leafing through the Yellow Pages to find the number of St Ives' police station.

5

It was just after five when Jack Curnow put his head around the door of Keith's office. Keith was making an effort to tidy up his paperwork, but like many such tasks, his room was looking more chaotic, not less at this particular stage.

'Sir,' Jack began. 'Blimey, what's going on here?'

'I'm having a tidy-up,' said Keith.

Jack grinned. 'Are you sure, sir?'

'Enough. Have you any news?'

'I have. Andy Symonds is definitely alive, he is married to a woman called Anne, lives in Sale, in Manchester and has two children.'

'And you are absolutely sure you've got the right bloke?'

'Completely, sir. He was born in Penzance to Violet and David Symonds, he grew up in Tanner's Cottage. Maybe she is a bit senile, the mother, I mean.'

'No,' said Keith, 'no she's not, she is absolutely

on the button. I don't know what she's playing at, but it's something to do with the victim I'll be bound. You couldn't try to trace the husband, could you? We know he went to Australia and he died some years ago.'

'I've done that sir, but he seems to have disappeared off the face of the earth, though that's not surprising given that he ran away to Australia rather inconveniently before computers recorded everything. I could try and make some enquiries over there. With the British embassy, perhaps.'

'No, don't let's go to that trouble yet,' said Keith, 'I need to go back and visit Violet Symonds. I'll do it first thing in the morning.' He glanced at his watch. 'I'll have to be leaving soon, I'm due to take Barbara out to supper tonight.'

'That'll be nice, sir, celebrating anything special?'

'No, not really, commiserating more like, trying to cheer her up about losing her job.'

'Her trip to Australia will do that, sir,' Jack said. 'You ought to be going.'

'Don't you start,' said Keith, warningly.

The young policeman had been very kind. He had accepted tea, made an appropriate fuss of Harvey, taken a description of the painting and luckily a photograph which Felicity suddenly remembered she had. It was of a long-ago Christmas in Oxford when the children were still very small – she and Charlie, Mel and James all standing grouped by the fire with the painting above their heads, well lit.

'This is most helpful, may I borrow it for a few days?'

Felicity nodded. 'Yes, of course, but it is a precious photograph, you see my husband is dead and…'

'I understand,' he said. 'I'll take great care of it, I promise.'

It was too late at night to call out a carpenter but between them they wedged the door shut. 'You could stay with a friend tonight if you would feel more comfortable, not that he will revisit the scene of the crime,' the policeman had said, firmly. 'He got what he came for. How many people knew you had such a valuable painting here in your home?'

Felicity shrugged her shoulders. 'Only my friends and family, casual visitors don't usually get further than the kitchen. This is where I sort of live, this is the room we sit in when visitors come because of the Aga,' and she indicated towards the French windows, 'and there is a little balcony out there where I spend a lot of time. The sitting room is nice but it's not a room I use very much.'

'So no casual visitor would know the painting was here, but clearly you must have told somebody who keeps bad company.'

'Or they told some one else. Any one of my friends or family could have mentioned it to somebody, who mentioned it to somebody else – where do you start trying to track down a thing like that?' There was a note of despair in her voice.

'We do get a lot of paintings back,' she was assured. 'We'll notify the dealers and the galleries to be on the lookout for it and in the meantime, I'll send somebody along in the morning to check for fingerprints, so seal off your sitting room if you don't mind and don't go in there.' He looked at her quizzically. 'The painting is insured, I assume?'

Felicity nodded. 'But that's not the point.'

'No, of course it's not. We'll ask around, this is a small town, there's a good chance somebody saw something.'

Felicity gave him a warm smile. 'Thank you very much, but it is a rough old night, I don't expect there were many people out and about.'

'We'll see what we can do, Mrs Paradise.'

On impulse Keith did not go straight home but drove instead to the Duchy Hospital. Miles was sitting up in bed reading a book and looking decidedly more perky.

'Oh no,' he said, 'now what have I done?'

'Nothing, nothing,' said Keith, smiling and

settling himself down in the chair beside the bed.

'No grapes then?'

'I don't know if you deserve any yet,' said Keith.

'I deserve a double helping,' said Miles.

'So you're going to see Anya?'

'I have seen her, and I'm going to see her again tomorrow.'

Keith smiled at the boy fondly. 'I am so pleased. How did it go?'

'It went very well.' Miles had the grace to blush slightly. 'You were right, she is absolutely stunning.'

'Told you,' said Keith. There was a moment's silence between them. 'Did she help?'

'Yes, she is starting to.'

Keith smiled at him. 'Starting to, eh? So you feel you need several visitations to feel completely better?'

Miles grinned. 'Yes, I think that probably about sums it up, Chief Inspector.'

'Good for you,' said Keith. 'Did she tell you anything about your sister you didn't know? I don't mean to pry, tell me to shut up if you want.'

'Not really,' said Miles, 'except that I think I had not appreciated how important I was in Marianna's life,' his face clouded, 'which makes it all the more terrible that I ran out on her that day.'

'Look, I've told you this many times,' said

Keith, 'and I'm going to repeat it just once more and then that's the end of it. If you had stayed you would have been killed as well as Marianna. I don't want to appear rude, but you're not exactly built to come off well in a fight. In all probability, in her last moments of life, Marianna would have either seen her beloved brother killed or would have died knowing that you were about to die. As it was, you ran away and that saved your life, and if Marianna could be in this room with us right now, she would get down on her knees and thank God you made that decision.' Keith was surprised at the strength of his own feelings. This boy had always got to him, always made him feel protective.

'Thanks,' Miles mumbled.

'How are things anyway?' Keith said, after a moment to relieve the emotion which seemed to be bouncing off the walls. 'Apart from the awfulness of the crash, are you getting on alright at home with your uncle?' He put a slight emphasis on the word and Miles looked up at him sharply.

'I'm allowed to do whatever I like now.' He hesitated. 'It is because my father is dead that I got to go to the Royal Academy. I'm no Yehudi Menuhin but I should be able to make a career out of my music and I love it,' he smiled. 'In fact I'm lost without it now. I asked mother to send a violin down here for me to practise, but the hospital have vetoed it.' He paused. 'I know you felt matters were unresolved,' he went on, 'but things are best left, I'm sorry if I...' His voice trailed away.

'I was warned off your case by MI5,' said Keith, 'there is nothing more I could have done. You don't need to apologise to me for anything.'

'I wasn't frank with you and you've been so kind to me, I didn't tell you the truth and you knew I'd lied. I hate that.' Miles plucked nervously at the sheet covering him, his head bowed.

'Do you want to tell me the truth now?' Keith asked, gently.

'I'd like to tell someone,' said Miles, 'but I don't know what you would do with the information. I know I can trust you as a friend, but you are a policeman, after all.'

'You can trust me, Miles,' said Keith, 'I was threatened with dismissal from the force if I didn't let the thing go. There is no way the case can be re-opened.'

Miles gazed out of the window avoiding eye-contact altogether. 'It was my uncle who died in the Serpentine,' he said, 'not my father. The man we buried was my uncle, the man masquerading as my uncle is my father.'

Keith let out a deep breath. 'I thought as much,' he said.

Miles turned to look at him. 'I knew you did

and I knew you realised what had happened.'

'And does anybody else suspect?'

'My mother and I know, of course, but no one else. My father had gone to great pains to distance himself from the business, he was getting close to retirement anyway. They were identical twins, my father and my uncle, so it was very difficult to tell the difference between them physically and, of course, no one working for us actually knew my "uncle" so the fact that he behaves so like my father is something people have just accepted.' Miles gave a sigh. 'But that is why he lets me do what I want, has agreed to me not going into the business, has allowed me to follow my own career in music. I told him I would tell you the truth if he didn't let me do what I wanted. Bribery and corruption I suppose, Chief Inspector, but it has allowed me to follow my dream.'

'And your mother, what does your mother think of it all?'

'My mother just wants a quiet life, she wants me to be happy and fulfilled and I am. In a strange kind of way I think she may have got her husband back. He's trapped in a way, trapped by both of us. We're not unkind to him, we don't threaten him in any way but he knows the power has shifted and so he has to behave better towards us than he used to. He's less of a tyrant, he treats us with more respect.'

'I suppose there is a link between you and your father now you have both lost siblings,' Keith suggested.

'Hardly, the circumstances are very different.'

'They were both killed within a few weeks of one another.'

'Yes, but my father deliberately put his brother in danger and doesn't appear to give a shit. I didn't know my sister was in danger and every day of my life I regret her death. I think, if anything, the contrast in our attitude towards our siblings drives us even further apart. The man is an absolute bastard, I'm forced to keep calling him Uncle Bob, but believe me that's a lot easier than calling him Father. I am deeply grateful that I am related to him in no way at all.'

'I can understand that,' said Keith, quietly.

Miles looked up at him, his face anguished. 'Have I done the wrong thing telling you all this, are you going to take it further, are you going to tell someone?'

'No,' said Keith, 'I gave you my word, your secret is completely safe with me.' He glanced at his watch. 'Oh, my God, I'm going to be in trouble with my wife, I am supposed to take her out to dinner in five minutes.'

'You'd better go then,' said Miles.

Keith stood up and walked towards the door.

'Have fun with Anya when you see her next.'

'Chief Inspector?'

Keith paused. 'Yes?'

'I would have liked to have had a dad like you, it has been such a relief being able to tell you the truth.'

Keith stood at the door. 'I'm very glad if it helped, Miles, and the feeling is mutual – that stupid bugger Hugo Irving masquerading as your uncle, should recognise what a lucky man he is to have a son like you.' They stared at one another for a moment and smiled.

'Don't forget my grapes next time you come,' said Miles.

'Dear God, is the boy never satisfied?' said Keith, as he walked off down the corridor.

In the car driving home through the dark wet streets of Truro, Keith's mind was full of the Irving family. There was nothing he could do, or would do, about the revelation Miles had just disclosed. A promise was a promise, and in any event he had been warned off the case by his boss, Superintendent Staple. Anything he did now would hurt a lot of people and probably get himself suspended. He knew he had the proof within his grasp. Hugo Irving's twin brother Bob, who had convicted of drink-driving some years earlier and his fingerprints were on file. While identical twins share the same DNA, they do not share the same fingerprints. 'But it would achieve nothing,' Keith said out loud and turned into his drive with a heavy heart, knowing he would be in trouble for being late – again.

6

The following morning Keith Penrose and his sergeant, Jack Curnow, drove into St Ives bright and early.

'I think I'll see Violet Symonds on my own if you wouldn't mind,' said Keith, 'I just have a feeling she is more likely to confide in me if I'm unaccompanied.'

'Why is that then sir, is it because I'm not the tactful type like you?'

'Enough cheek, young Curnow, I have a way with old ladies.'

'If you say so, sir,' said Jack. 'I'll drop you in Bedford Road. Will you give me a ring when you're through?'

'I will,' said Keith.

Violet took a long time to answer the door.

'Sorry dear,' she said, as though she was expecting him. 'My arthritis is playing up today, it's this damp. Come along in, I'll put the kettle on.

You'd like a nice cup of tea, wouldn't you?'

Keith followed her snail's pace into the kitchen and decided not to wait for the tea to be made this time. He sat down at her kitchen table.

'We now have more information on the skeleton at Tanner's Cottage.'

'Oh yes,' she said, conversationally.

'The victim was a male, late forties or early fifties, about five foot eleven and used to manual labour.'

'That's interesting.' She had her back to him as she busied herself with the teapot so he could not see her expression.

'Do you want to know how he died? I don't want to upset you,' he asked.

'Well, I expect you want to tell me.'

'He was hit on the head and then shot.'

She turned around. 'Shot, what with a gun?'

'Yes, a gun,' said Keith, patiently. 'Why, are you surprised?'

She turned back to the teapot. 'No, no, of course not, it's just that I can't imagine anybody shooting anybody in St Erth.'

'It happened in the late 1970s,' Keith went on, 'during the time you lived in the cottage. It seems a little odd, doesn't it?'

'Does it?' Violet said, bringing the teapot to the table. Her hand was shaking but then, at her age, that did not necessarily mean anything. She looked particularly frail this morning.

'Well yes,' said Keith, 'a man gets shot and buried in your garden during the time you lived there, and you know nothing about it?'

'That's right, dear, I know absolutely nothing about it. They must have buried the body at night, not a pleasant thought.'

'And you wouldn't have been surprised by the freshly-dug earth in the morning?'

'As I said, while my husband was still at home we had a vegetable patch too, out the back. It was only after he was gone, I let it grow out and put down a bit of grass seed.'

Keith moved on. 'There is another thing, Mrs Symonds, your son Andrew, you told me he'd died in a motorcycle accident, but he's not dead is he? He lives with his wife, Anne, and your two grandchildren in Sale, just outside Manchester. Why did you tell me he was dead?'

'I didn't say he was dead, I said he was in a motorcycle accident when he was a teenager, and he was.' Violet's expression assumed a mulish look and she was avoiding eye-contact.

'He might have been,' said Keith, 'but he didn't die in that accident, did he?'

Violet didn't reply. She poured the tea and pushed the cup and saucer in Keith's direction.

'Did he?' Keith repeated.

'No,' Violet said, 'but he might as well have done.'

'What do you mean?' Keith asked.

'Married this upmarket girl from Cheshire – a big country house her parents live in, very posh. He was ashamed of me, Andy that is, he calls himself Andrew now. They didn't want anything to do with me, not once they married. I have only seen the children once when they came on holiday and spent a day in St Ives. The children didn't seem to think much of me either. I was glad to see the back of them.'

'I'm so sorry,' said Keith, and he was. 'I can quite understand what a difficult situation it must be for you, particularly with your husband gone, but I still don't understand why you told me Andy was dead.'

Violet's mouth went into a thin line of disapproval. 'Like I said, he is dead to me.' They drank their tea in silence for a few minutes. Violet seemed to have turned in on herself and was staring down stubbornly at the table.

'So you have absolutely no idea who the man in your garden might have been?' Keith repeated.

'No I haven't,' Violet said, 'as I've told you already. It's not my fault some skeleton fetches up in the house I used to live in.'

'I'm not saying it is your fault,' Keith said, 'it just seems odd that a body could have ended up in your back garden without any member of your family knowing about it.'

'Maybe we were on holiday when it happened,' Violet said.

'Maybe,' Keith agreed. 'You sounded surprised when I said that the man had been shot, why was that?'

'Like I said, we don't have shootings in this part of the world, do we?'

'Not normally,' Keith agreed, 'but I do have to identify the victim. He is some mother's son, or some wife's husband, some child's father – they may think that he abandoned them. People need to know, people need closure when someone dies, besides which it looks like a murder has been committed. I have to identify the person and find out who put him in the ground.' He stood up. 'Thank you for the tea. If you think of anything,' he put his card on the table, 'just give me a ring, yes?' He walked to the door. 'What did your husband do before he went off to Australia?'

Violet looked up at him. 'He...' she hesitated, 'he worked on a farm. I suppose you'd say he was a farm labourer. He wanted a place of his own but could never afford one down here. I think it's one of the reasons he went to Australia.'

'Right, thank you Mrs Symonds. Don't move, I'll see myself out.'

Jack had found a parking space in Bedford Road and was waiting for him when he came out.

'Any luck?' he asked Keith.

'Not really,' said Keith, 'she is hiding something, she went all shifty on me and she was definitely surprised that the victim had been shot, suggesting she has some knowledge of what happened. I'm just wondering if the victim is actually her husband and that he never went to Australia.'

'I'll see what I can find out about him,' said Jack. 'There must be some record of him applying for Australian visas and possibly citizenship, he must have needed work permits and all sorts. I'll get onto the embassy and see what they can do to help.'

'I think that would be a good idea. We need to establish if the man really did run off and that he didn't end up back in his own vegetable patch. We need the son interviewed and a DNA sample taken. Right, let's go back to the station.'

'Just a moment,' said Jack. 'I went in to have a chat with the local boys while I was waiting. There was a burglary in town last night.'

'Oh yes,' said Keith, obviously far from interested.

'A very valuable painting was stolen, a Constable.'

Keith's head snapped up. 'Not from...'

'Yes, from Felicity Paradise's house. Do you want to go and take a look?'

'Yes,' said Keith, 'yes, I definitely do.'

Keith arrived just as a member of the scene of crime team was leaving.

'Any luck?' he asked, showing the man his warrant card. They were standing outside Felicity's ruined front door.

'Not much, sir, I suspect there is just the one set of prints which I imagine will be Mrs Paradise's, they're all over the house, but I very much doubt the intruder will have left any trace. A professional job, if ever I saw one.'

'Right then, I'll go upstairs and see Mrs Paradise,' said Keith, starting up the stairs.

'One thing sir,' he called, 'this isn't the first one, in my view.'

'This isn't the first what?' Keith stopped and turned back to the man.

'The theft of a valuable painting. There was a painting, just a single one like this, taken from a house in Carbis Bay last week. I did the job there too, very similar, no disturbance, he knew exactly what he was looking for.'

'Was that a Constable too?'

'I don't know, I'm not the detective, but I reckon it was the same fellow.'

'Thanks,' said Keith.

Felicity was sitting forlornly at the kitchen table surrounded by paperwork as Keith bounded up the stairs and arrived in the kitchen, unannounced.

'Keith!' she said, looking up. 'I'm so pleased to see you.' She jumped up and made as if to hug him and then clearly thought better of it. 'Would you like a cup of coffee?'

'I'd love one,' he said.

'How come you're here, do you know about the burglary?'

'Yes,' said Keith.

'How?'

'My spies. No, actually, I was interviewing again in Bedford Road and Jack heard about it from the boys at the Station, so I thought I would pop around and see how you are.'

'Is Jack here too, does he want a coffee?'

Keith shook his head. 'No, he's staying in the car to do battle with the Australian embassy.'

'Good Lord,' said Felicity, 'are you off to see Carly then?'

'No,' said Keith, 'but Barbara's going next week.' There was a moment's awkward pause. It was impossible for either of them to ignore the implications of Barbara's absence. After a moment, Keith cleared his throat. 'I'm following up the Australian embassy on quite a different matter, connected with my skeleton in St Erth,' he managed.

'Oh I see,' said Felicity, faintly.

'Battling with insurance by the look of it?' Keith said, nodding at the papers strewn across the kitchen table.

'Yes, they are not too pleased, there is going to be an awful fuss about it.'

'Why?' he asked.

'Such a valuable painting, apparently it should have been burglar-alarmed and all sorts.'

'I suppose it should,' said Keith.

'I think the general feeling is that I have behaved very irresponsibly and I realise I have, but I can't live in a house that's locked up all the time. When I go into town I often don't lock my front door at all, I never thought it was a problem.'

'Locking the front door didn't stop this chap coming in anyway, did it?' Keith said.

'No, but an alarm might have. I told you, didn't I, the story of this painting?'

Keith nodded. 'As soon as they mentioned that a Constable was missing I had a terrible feeling that it was yours, there can't be too many people with a painting of that calibre in St Ives.'

'Except in the Tate.'

'Except in the Tate,' Keith agreed. 'I'd better make sure they are aware of your theft, they may want to beef up security. Another valuable painting was taken in Carbis Bay last week apparently.'

'Oh, do you have any details?' Felicity asked.

'No, I've only just found out from the scene of crime officer downstairs. He reckons it's the same villain – smashed the door down, walked in, knew where he was going, knew what he wanted, took it and was gone. No messing.'

'It's a horrible thought,' Felicity shuddered.

'I know, I'm sorry. It must have been rotten for you and you must have been very frightened when you came home. I hope you called the police before you went into the house to investigate.'

Felicity grinned at him. 'No, of course not, I did it the other way round.'

'Yes, of course you did,' said Keith, 'silly of me to even suggest it.' They smiled warmly at one another.

'Here's your coffee,' said Felicity, putting it on the Aga beside him. 'Can we talk about something other than this painting? I'm so upset about it, I haven't even dared tell the children yet.'

'I suppose they see it as their inheritance?'

Felicity nodded. 'I agreed with them a long

time ago that James would have it and that if he or Mel were ever in trouble, they could sell it and split the proceeds.'

'You can give them the insurance money, I suppose,' said Keith.

'If I ever get it. I hate insurance companies.' They drank their coffee in silence for a moment.

'So, if you've nothing more to tell me about your skeleton, tell me about Miles. Has he given in and seen Anya yet?'

Keith grinned. 'Yes,' he said, 'result! Not only have they met once, but they're meeting again. He seems to be very taken with her. She is a lovely girl.'

'I was thinking about Miles the other day and wondering, has he ever admitted to you the true identity of the twin who is living the life of Uncle Bob?'

Felicity Paradise had a nasty habit of doing this to him, he thought, as he covered his confusion by another sip of coffee. She had an uncanny knack of putting her finger right on the pulse.

'You know my views on the subject,' he said, trying to deflect her.

'Yes,' she said, patiently, 'I know your views, Keith, but I just wondered whether Miles has ever said anything, ever told you the truth. He must know there is nothing you can do about it, not now.'

'Miles has got more sense than to start confiding in anyone,' Keith said.

'But you're not anyone, are you Keith, and you're batting back the answers to my questions but you're actually telling me nothing.'

Keith met her eyes and smiled. 'That's entirely right,' he said.

'And that's how it's going to stay?'

He nodded. 'Sorry.'

'That's OK, as long as Miles is doing alright. It's just typical that he was in this awful car crash and lost his friends. He is a child of storm, isn't he?'

'He is rather,' Keith acknowledged, 'but a plucky one. Life has dealt him a very peculiar hand but he seems to be coping with it rather well.'

'You're very fond of him, aren't you?' Felicity said.

'Yes,' Keith admitted, 'I am. I think it was going to Romania, seeing the country, listening to his description of the orphanage. It is only four hours away by air and yet it is like moving into Dickensian England.'

'You've always been an old softie where children are concerned,' Felicity observed. 'So, tell me, why aren't you going to Australia too?'

Keith shrugged his shoulders. 'I don't know, there is quite a lot going on here at the moment. I also feel Carly has hardly been gone five minutes and we need to give her a bit of space.'

'I'm sure she would love to see her old Dad,' Felicity said.

'Less of the old, please.'

'Sorry,' said Felicity, 'but you two have always been so close.'

'I know, I know,' said Keith. 'I think the truth is …' he hesitated.

'Go on,' said Felicity.

'I think if we go out there, it's going to show how easy it is for us to visit and it is going to encourage her to stay there. If we stay away then maybe she will come home.'

'Or seeing you might make her recognise what she is missing?' Felicity suggested.

Keith shook his head. 'I don't know, I just feel that I shouldn't be going now so I'm not and Barbara seems to be quite happy to go on her own, after initially being cross with me. Anyway, enough of my idiocy, I'd better get going. I'll put a bit of muscle behind this burglary and find out about the other one in Carbis Bay, see if we've got a pattern. If we have, then this guy needs to be stopped, and fast.'

'Thanks,' said Felicity. She stood up too and they stared at one another for a long poignant moment. Keith leant forward and kissed her briefly on the cheek and then belted down the stairs without another word.

7

Detective Inspector Richard Fairfield of Manchester CID interviewed Andrew Symonds on Friday evening in his luxury Victorian house in Sale. The interview took place in the conservatory which was built in the same style as the house and must have cost a fortune. Having refused a Scotch, DI Fairfield accepted a glass of carbonated water, which was delivered in a frosted glass with ice and a slice of lime.

'This is a lovely house, sir,' he said, in an attempt to ingratiate himself. His companion was not amused.

'Detective Inspector Fairfield, I've had a long day, it's Friday and I want to relax with my wife and children. If you have anything to say could you please say it now. I am, I have to say, in no mood for small talk.'

'I'm sorry, sir,' said Richard Fairfield, already starting to hate this guy. 'I'm interviewing you at the request of Devon and Cornwall Constabulary.'

'Is this about my mother, is she in some kind of trouble?'

'No, it's not about your mother,' Richard replied, 'at least, not directly. It's about the house you grew up in, Tanner's Cottage.'

'What about it?'

'A body, or rather a skeleton, has been found in the back garden of the cottage.'

'I see.' Richard Fairfield watched the man closely. There was no obvious sign of distress nor did he show particular surprise. 'And what has that got to do with us?'

'The body has been there since 1978 or possibly 1979 when you and your mother, and indeed your father, were all still living there.'

'So you're asking whether one of us buried somebody in the garden?'

'I suppose I am, sir.'

'Well I was only, what, about sixteen at the time, I wasn't in the habit of going around burying people in the garden.'

'And your father, was he a violent man?' Richard enquired.

'He was a bastard,' Andrew said, 'but I don't think he was a killer, no.'

'Why a bastard?' Richard enquired.

'He was not good to my mother.'

'And then, of course, he ran off, didn't he, with

95

someone, I gather he emigrated to Australia?'

'That's about it,' Andrew said. 'Now, if you have no more questions…'

'I still have a few, sir,' Richard said, firmly. 'When my colleague in Cornwall first interviewed your mother, she said you'd been killed in a motorcycle accident when you were a teenager. Why would she have said that, sir?'

'Because we're estranged, we never see each other.'

'And may I ask why that is?'

'My wife and my mother don't get along well and my mother and I have nothing in common.'

'Still, you're her only child and with your father gone, she's all alone, and with respect, getting on a bit now.'

'Look Detective Inspector, I do not need you to start lecturing me about family values. My mother and I are quite comfortable with our relationship, we know exactly where we both stand and it is no one's damn business, especially not yours.'

'Just a couple of other questions then, sir,' said Richard, determined not to appear ruffled. 'Did your father have a vegetable garden when he still lived at Tanner's Cottage?'

Andrew frowned. 'Yes, as far as I know.'

'And did you go on growing vegetables after he

left?'

Andrew shook his head. 'No, my mother hadn't the time and I wasn't interested. We just let it grow over.'

'Because you didn't fancy digging around a dead body?'

Andrew Symonds leapt to his feet as Richard had known he would. 'How dare you! What are you insinuating? I don't have to sit here and listen to this, I want you out of my house right now.'

'I'm on my way, sir,' said DI Fairfield, 'but there is just one more thing, sir.'

'What!' shouted Andrew Symonds.

'We'd like you to come down to the station at your convenience and provide a DNA sample.'

'Why in God's name should I do that?' Andrew Symonds demanded.

'So that we can eliminate one possibility from our enquiries.'

'And what would that be?' Andrew said, his voice rising yet another decibel.

'We need to make sure that the body isn't that of your father.'

Felicity was sitting on a bench on the Island looking out towards Godrevy lighthouse. It was a cold clear day but there was no wind. Harvey was rooting around on the rocks below her and clearly very happy with his lot. Felicity, by contrast, was feeling miserable and guilty. She had just switched off her phone after a protracted conversation with Mel, in which she had confessed the loss of the Constable. Mel had been full of recriminations – why hadn't the painting been put in the bank, or given to James whose house was properly secure?

'What would Dad have thought?' Mel said, twisting the knife in the wound. 'It was his most precious possession, 'The Insurance' he called it. He knew if any of us were ever up against it, the Constable would see us through.'

'I know Dad wouldn't have wanted me to put it into the bank,' said Felicity, showing some spirit at last, 'he thought the painting should be enjoyed.'

'Well at least we'll get the insurance money, I suppose.' There was a disturbing silence. 'It was insured, Mum?' Mel said, her voice rising with obvious panic.

'Yes,' said Felicity, 'yes it was insured and for the correct amount, but the insurance company are quibbling.'

'Insurance companies always quibble,' said Mel.

'No, this is more serious Mel, apparently I should have had the picture alarmed and the house alarmed, it's part of the insurance requirements.'

'So why didn't you?' Mel said, clearly aghast at

her mother's stupidity.

'Because it wasn't alarmed in Oxford,' said Felicity. Your father would never have managed to get in and out of the house if we'd had an alarm system. As you know, the picture just lived in his study, over the mantelpiece so I simply brought it here and did the same thing, put it over the mantelpiece.'

'Times change Mother,' Mel said. 'I just can't believe you did this, we've always had that picture to fall back on.'

'Oh Mel, stop,' said Felicity. 'I'm feeling so guilty as it is, not so much about your inheritance, but for the sake of Charlie's mother who clearly loved the painting. I can't turn the clock back though, what's happened has happened.'

James was altogether kinder, when Felicity called him a fw moments later. 'Don't worry Mum,' he said, 'I'm sure someone will track it down for you in the end, though it might take a while – a few months or even years. If the police don't have any luck, we could always try one of those art theft investigators.'

'That sounds expensive,' said Felicity.

'Maybe, maybe not, just don't worry about it for the moment. It must have been an awful shock for you.'

Felicity felt a little tearful at so much kindness

and blinked hurriedly, focusing her eyes on the horizon beyond Godrevy lighthouse. 'It wasn't nice Jamie, you're right. It is horrible somebody breaking into your house for a start and then, that painting, it meant so much to your father and grandmother, it was the link with her past.'

'I know,' said Jamie.

'Mel said I should have kept it in the bank or given it to you.'

'Rubbish,' said Jamie, 'Dad would be doing handsprings in his grave if he thought you had put in the bank. Who can enjoy a painting when it's in the bank, for God's sake?'

'That's what I thought,' said Felicity, gratefully. 'Tell me, on a more cheerful note, how are the boys?'

Felicity's grandsons, Sam and Harry, were eleven and nine respectively. She adored them both, of course, but Harry, the younger, had inherited much from her late husband, Charlie – the same floppy flaxen hair, the same twinkle in his blue eyes, the same sense of humour – he had a special place in her heart.

'They're both good,' Jamie said, 'driving us mad, of course. They are so busy all the time – Trish and I spend our entire lives in the car driving them to this match or that practice session – they're both so sporty, unlike me.'

'You have other skills,' said Felicity, firmly. Jamie had been a great worry to her as a little boy. He was constantly outshone by his very competent younger sister. It was only when he discovered his gift for IT that gradually he had emerged from his shell. 'I do miss you,' Felicity said, suddenly.

'Well, we'll be down for Christmas, won't we, Ma? Not long now – the boys are very excited. It's going to be bedlam.'

'Yes it is, but fun.'

'I love you Mum and don't worry, not even for a moment. We'll sort this out and if you want me to deal with the insurance company, just e-mail me their details and I'll do some shouting – or better still, I'll put Trish on the case.'

'Thank you Jamie, I'll try and deal with it myself but if I'm getting nowhere I really would appreciate your help. Love you, too.'

Felicity stood up and whistled to Harvey and together they continued around the Island and down the steps onto Porthmeor beach. The tide was way out but the wind was blowing in from the harbour side of town so it was quite sheltered and she was wearing her wellies. 'Come on Harvey, let's go down to the sea.' They walked slowly out towards the breakers; the beach was a mass of pools left by the sea and Harvey who was rather fastidious about getting his feet wet, took great detours around them. 'Sissy!' Felicity called to him.

The clarity of the light was amazing, the definition extraordinary, it could only be St Ives. To her left, Man's Head, that strange crop of rock which earned its name from how it looked, provided a startling profile and looking back at the town, the Tate Gallery gleamed brightly in the morning light. Charlie had always enjoyed the architecture of the building so close to the beach. How long ago now it was since she had lived in Oxford, how long ago it felt since Charlie was alive. Standing now, way out on Porthmeor beach, looking towards the Island and then sweeping her gaze right around past the Tate and up towards Clodgey, only emphasised the wisdom of her decision. Her Achilles heel, of course, was Jamie, Trish and the boys. She had seen so much more of them when she lived in Oxford, and she missed them terribly but this was her home now, she couldn't ever imagine going back.

Felicity and Harvey retraced their steps across the beach and walked down Bunkers Hill towards Fore Street. Felicity glanced at her watch; she was due to deliver some paintings to the Penzance gallery. If she was going to be on time she needed to get a move on. Jamie's words had calmed her; it was time to move on from the theft, accept it and live with it.

The Windward Gallery, just off Chapel Street in Penzance was an attractive building. The window had a deep bow to it and the wooden window frames were varnished like an old ship. The name of the gallery was burnt onto a piece of driftwood which hung over the door. It was only a small space from which to sell their stock of paintings, prints and cards but the gallery owner, Tom Ward, had told Felicity there was plenty of storage at the back and he and his girlfriend, Sarah, lived over the shop so it was ideal for them.

Tom was alone in the shop when Felicity staggered in clutching her six canvases. He strode across the gallery and took them from her. 'Wow, you've been hard at work.'

'Six is what you said you wanted and six is what you've got,' said Felicity.

Tom carried them over to the counter and laid them down. 'Let's have a look,' he said. He studied each painting carefully, nodding with approval. 'They're great,' he said, 'we'll have no trouble getting rid of those. Well done.'

'I can't believe you're selling so many when things are so quiet at the moment.'

'Building up to Christmas, I suppose,' said Tom. 'Paintings at a sensible price, which yours are, but unusual and unique in their own way, are just the sort of thing people are looking for. I'll call

Sarah, she'd love to see you. Would you like a glass of wine?'

Felicity hesitated. 'Well, just the one, I'm driving.'

'OK, I'll call her.'

Felicity watched as Tom bounded up the stairs to the flat above. He was an attractive man, in his early forties she imagined, but he dressed in a totally inappropriate way for West Cornwall. He looked like a tailor's dummy with his neatly-pressed trousers, his sharp shirts and matching cravats. She could understand how he fitted in to life in Islington which is where he and Sarah had come from, but he looked hugely out of place here. Maybe though, that was a strength, making him different. He came back down the stairs clutching a bottle.

'It's only a Cava, I'm afraid, but it's a good one. We can't afford proper champagne except on very, very special occasions.'

'Goodness,' said Felicity, 'some fizz, are we celebrating something?'

'No, not really, other than the fact that we are entertaining one of our favourite artists, who is selling really well.'

'She is too,' said Sarah, leaping down the stairs and into sight. She was younger than Tom, probably in her late thirties, with a mane of shiny blonde hair, beautiful skin and a wonderful figure. She was not strictly speaking beautiful or even particularly pretty, but her glowing good health and apparently boundless energy made her very attractive. She rushed across the room and kissed Felicity on both cheeks. 'Congratulations, you're selling so well, we're really grateful.'

'Not half as grateful as I am,' said Felicity, 'it's so great to find a regular outlet for my work.' Tom popped the cork, poured the Cava and they all raised their glasses in a toast. 'So how long have you two been down here?' Felicity said. 'As you know, I only found your gallery a few months ago.'

'About eighteen months,' said Tom, 'and we absolutely love it.'

'It must be a huge change after London,' Felicity said, 'Islington, wasn't it?'

'Yes, it's certainly been an eye-opener and there have been a lot of adjustments to make, but it's a very beautiful part of the world and so relaxed.' Sarah was wearing high boots, leggings and a smock top in various shades of brown. She didn't look very West Cornwall either, Felicity thought.

'Do you see yourselves making a long-term future down here?' she asked, curiously.

Tom shrugged. 'We'll see how it goes, but we've no plans to go anywhere else at the moment. What about you, have you always lived here?'

Felicity shook her head. 'Only seven years. My husband died rather suddenly, I just needed a change. The children were all grown up and I ended up here, well not here exactly, in St Ives as you know.'

'And you're happy with the move?' Sarah asked.

'Yes, I am,' said Felicity. 'I've just been thinking about it, strangely enough. I had a walk on Porthmeor beach before I came over to you. My son, my elder child, lives up in Oxfordshire and while I used to see him and his family all the time, I see them somewhat infrequently now. They're coming down for Christmas but it's not the same as being able to pop in.'

'And you regret that?' Tom asked.

'Yes of course I regret it, but it doesn't make any difference, I couldn't live anywhere else but here now.'

'How interesting,' said Tom, 'why is that?'

Felicity took a sip of her wine and pondered the question. 'It's got under my skin, it's where I belong. I walk down Fore Street in the morning, out of season of course, and I know nearly everyone and nearly everyone knows me. There is time to stop for a chat... and then, of course, there is the sea. Having grown up in Oxfordshire, where you are as far away from the coast as you can get, the sea is something of a luxury. I don't think I would leave the sea now.' She smiled at them both. 'I think I'm stuck with St Ives and the town is stuck with me. Because of all the visitors it is easy to forget in summer but in reality, it's just a small town, a very special small town.'

Tom smiled. 'Your eloquence certainly suggests you're going nowhere, Felicity.'

Driving home to St Ives after her meeting with Tom and Sarah, something niggled at the back of Felicity's mind. She liked them both very much and they had been nothing but kind and enthusiastic about her work. They were proving to be good friends, yet there was something not quite right, something just out of reach. It wasn't until she and Harvey were walking down the narrow streets from Barnoon that the thought struck her. She had sat with Tom and Sarah for over an hour during the lunch-time period and not a single person had come into their gallery, nor even hovered around the window looking as though they might be interested; the place had been absolutely dead. So how were they selling so many of her paintings? It was Friday, which she knew from conversations with art galleries in St Ives was a difficult day, when people went food shopping and prepared for the weekend rather than wandering round galleries.

Nonetheless, it was hard to see how they were managing to shift so many of her paintings. Why was their gallery doing so well when all the other galleries Felicity had approached were not interested in taking new stock at this time of the year? It was slightly odd.

8

'He's an awful prat,' DI Richard Fairfield was saying to Keith Penrose the following Monday morning.

Keith laughed down the phone. 'So is that your formal verdict?'

'Not exactly, I've e-mailed a report to you, but honestly the man is an idiot, pumped up with his own self-importance, a complete wally.'

'That's odd,' said Keith, 'because his mother is not at all like that. A sweet old thing really, at least I hope she is, it's certainly how she presents. It is why I want to shifty around and dig out as much information as I can, rather than confront her until we do have to do so.'

'Do you think the mother is a killer then?' asked Richard.

'I find it hard to believe,' said Keith, after a pause, 'but she's lied to me once, so I suppose she could lie to me again. There is something slightly odd about her.'

'Odd in what way?' Richard asked.

'I'm not sure,' said Keith 'It just feels she's not quite telling it how it is.'

'DNA samples are winging their way to you now,' Richard said. 'Even if Andy Symonds is out of the frame, I'd still like to know how this one ends – will you keep me informed?'

'I certainly will,' said Keith, 'and thanks so much for your help.'

'Would you like me to give you a brief lecture on how long it takes to process DNA results?' Horace said, in immediate response to Keith's telephone call.

'I know how long it takes,' Keith said, 'because I've been on the receiving end of that particular lecture any number of times, and very interesting it is too, Horace – every time I hear it.'

'I'm glad you're so appreciative,' said Horace. 'As to how quickly I can get you the results of a possible DNA match depends very largely on whether a fellow is allowed to get on with his job.'

It had been decided that as Barbara's flight on Tuesday was shortly after midday with a three-hour check-in, they should travel up to Heathrow on Monday afternoon. Keith had reckoned it was the moment to splash out and so had booked them into a 5-star hotel near Heathrow and reserved a table in the restaurant. They arrived shortly after seven, and having checked in, had drinks around a rather exotic indoor pool, complete with palms and floodlights and a cocktail bar in the centre. Keith thought the whole thing unbearably pretentious but he could see that Barbara was appreciating it, and he was glad. Dinner of course was overpriced but adequate. Barbara was friendly enough but there was a certain tension in the air.

'Are you worried about flying all that distance on your own?' Keith asked over coffee.

Barbara looked up at him, surprised. 'No, not at all. I can't wait, what an adventure! As you know I've never been outside Europe before and with a stop over in Singapore, it'll be marvellous.'

Keith was genuinely surprised by her enthusiasm. They had lived together for so many years but in many respects, Keith realised, they did not know each other all that well. He had spent his entire marriage preoccupied with his work, she with the children and then her job; holidays had been infrequent and when they had managed a few days away, Keith spent most of them sleeping. It was strange to know someone so well and yet in another way, hardly at all. He would have imagined her to be nervous, or at least apprehensive about taking off across to the other side of the world all alone.

'What have I said to offend you, then?' Barbara

asked, into the silence that had followed her obvious enthusiasm.

'Nothing, why?'

'You've gone all quiet on me.'

Keith struggled – the need to communicate suddenly seemed rather urgent. They were going to be parted for six weeks; they had never been away from each other before for more than a few days. 'I was just thinking that after all these years, you still have the ability to surprise me – the way you've taken to the idea of your trip to Australia, your enthusiasm. I'd have thought you would have been quite, well, apprehensive about it, I suppose.'

'Why, because I haven't got you to keep me company?' Barbara challenged him.

'No...' Keith hesitated. 'No, not exactly, not me particularly, but having someone to travel with would make the whole thing less daunting, wouldn't it?'

'Keith, since the day we married there's been a whole lot of things I've had to cope with on my own – when the children weren't well, when in the early days we had no money and I was trying to balance the books – I've done it all on my own.'

'I don't think that's entirely fair,' Keith said.

'Believe me,' said Barbara, 'if you've tried to manhandle two tiny children and a buggy on and off a bus in the dark, in the rush hour, one not well, both past their bedtimes, trying to get to the doctor's surgery before it closes; not being able to afford a taxi and recognising that your husband is not going to be home in time to help – if you've been through that sort of thing, not once but many times, sitting back in a seat being waited on hand and foot and watching a film while flying halfway across the world, is a piece of cake.'

'Are you always going to hold it against me,' Keith said, 'my commitment to my job?'

Barbara studied him in silence for a moment. 'Yes, I am,' she said, without a trace of emotion.

Keith felt and looked crestfallen. 'It's not the type of job you can do part-time,' he began.

'I don't want to talk about your job tonight, Keith. You asked the question you probably shouldn't have done, and maybe I should have been more tactful in my answer. The fact is though, you missed years of involvement in the children's lives and years of any possible life we might have had together as a married couple. I've spent so many hours hanging around, waiting for you to turn up, listening to the same old excuse over and over again. For once, it feels really good that it's me who is going away and you who's staying put.'

The waiter glided by. Keith summoned him. 'I think I'll have a brandy, would you like one?'

'Why not?' said Barbara, 'It's a holiday after

113

all.'

'I don't want us to part on bad terms,' Keith said, when the waiter had gone.

'Nor do I, Keith. I'm just telling you how it is.'

Keith frowned at her. 'It's strange, you're sort of different, I can't put my finger on it exactly.'

'What, you, the great student of human nature?'

He chose to ignore the sarcasm. 'What is it, what is different about you?'

Barbara considered the question. 'I feel free,' she said.

'Should I be upset by that?' Keith asked.

'No,' said Barbara, 'you should be happy for me. You're a nice man underneath it all, you should be happy about the place in which I find myself.' Their brandies arrived.

'What place?' Keith asked.

'I'm back in charge of my life,' said Barbara, 'no job, but a bit of money in the bank, no children to care for – I can do what I like, go where I please, which is why I'm off to Australia.'

'And do I fit into this new place?' Keith asked.

Barbara studied him in silence for a moment. 'I don't know, Keith. I don't know what is going to become of you in a few years' time when you stop being a policeman. To be honest, I don't know how you'll cope, but whatever you do I can't imagine you living away from Cornwall. How I see it is this – I'm going to sort out what I want and what is right for me and I don't feel guilty about that because I think it is my turn to put myself first. When I've done that, we'll see whether you fit in to my life, or indeed whether you want to fit in to it.'

'You don't mince your words do you, my girl?' Keith said, ruefully raising his brandy glass to her.

'I didn't want to speak about this tonight,' said Barbara, 'but you raised it.'

'I'm glad we did,' said Keith, 'I'm glad we cleared the air. I want you to be happy in whatever you do and I also want you to know that although you think I've been a lousy husband and father, I am very grateful to you for all the years of care you devoted to both me and the children.'

'I believe that's true,' was all Barbara would say; 'now let's talk about arrangements for tomorrow.'

Tuesday was one of Felicity's 'granny days'. Looking after her granddaughter, Minty, who was now three and a half, had been a doddle, she now realised. She and Minty liked the same things – swimming, drawing, walking on the beach – and as a baby, Minty had been positively angelic. Fourteen-month-old Charlie was a completely different kettle of fish. He was a glorious-looking baby with flaxen hair, big blue eyes and the cherubic face of a choir boy. In reality he was a monster. He was totally fixated on his mother and really no one else in the world would do, so when he was parted from her he screamed – a lot. On this particular Tuesday, Charlie had been sick in the night, he was teething and suffering from lack of sleep and had clung to his mother like a limpet when Felicity tried to drag him away from her as Mel went to work.

'I'll try to come home early,' Mel mouthed above the din of Charlie's screams, but from the experience of being married to a lawyer, Felicity knew the chances of that were slim.

It was a cold, dank day, raining intermittently and blowing a gale – there was no question of taking the children outside. Felicity and Minty tried everything to entertain Charlie, but he was not to be pacified. In desperation, Felicity plonked him on a beanbag in front of CBeebies while she made a plan.

'So what are we going to do, Minty?' she said, regarding her granddaughter, whom from a very early age she had treated as an equal. Minty expected nothing less from grown-ups – she was very bright and articulate like her mother had been, but she was softer, kinder, Felicity had to admit.

Minty frowned. 'He sleeps in his car seat.'

'I'll tell you what we'll do,' said Felicity, 'we'll

put him in the car and we'll drive very slowly into St Ives and...'

'We'll go and see Annie,' they finished together.

'A plan,' said Felicity, 'wonderful. Let's find some coats.'

Pre-warned by a phone call, Annie Trethewey was waiting for them in her basement kitchen with hot chocolate at the ready and a plate of homemade scones. Well into her eighties now, Annie was as sharp as ever. There was a bird-like quality about her; she was very small and fine-boned with bright little eyes and even her white wispy hair was like soft baby bird down. Woken from his brief sleep, Charlie was howling again and without a word Annie took him from Felicity's arms.

A piece of kitchen roll was efficiently employed to clean the accumulation of tears and snot from Charlie's red face. Annie sat down on the kitchen chair and thrust a piece of scone into Charlie's chubby fingers. Immediately he leant back against her, a look of supreme contentment on his face as he began munching at the scone.

Felicity turned to Minty. 'It's amazing isn't it, we've been struggling all morning, haven't we Minty?'

'We have,' said Minty, 'and all he's done is

scream. It's why we came to you, Annie.'

'And there was me thinking you'd come to see me for my good company and really it's just so you could hand over this baby. Hot chocolate is on the Aga there and the tea is brewing, could you be mother, Felicity?' Annie turned her attention to Minty. 'You look proper bonny, Minty.'

'I am proper bonny,' Minty agreed, 'but Charlie's not, he was sick in the night and he's teething.'

'Who wouldn't scream with a toothache? I do. Do you want to get the paper and crayons out while Granny makes the drinks, you know where they are?'

Minty slid off her chair and went to the kitchen cupboard which housed a variety of toys, puzzles and crayons. A few moments later she was absorbed in a colouring book and Charlie had fallen fast asleep, snuggled into the crook of Annie's arm.

'How do you do it?' said Felicity, nodding towards the children.

'Years of practice, my girl.'

'Yes, I know, but I have four grandchildren, I should be pretty good at this by now. You look great, Annie, how are you?'

'I'm fine, but how are you? I heard you had a spot of bother.'

Felicity frowned. 'What do you mean?'

'Your burglary. I gather you lost that painting, what was it – a Constable, is that right?'

'Annie, how on earth do you know about that?'

Annie simply smiled at her.

'Sorry,' said Felicity, 'jungle telegraph, stupid, no one can have a secret in St Ives, not for long.'

'Why don't you want anyone to know?' Annie asked.

'The police think it is better to keep the press away from it at the moment. There's been another theft in Carbis Bay, also a valuable painting. It's not a secret, we're just not going to the press about it in a big way – yet, anyway.'

'Have they got any leads?' Annie asked.

'Not that I know of,' said Felicity.

'Isn't your inspector in charge then?'

'No,' said Felicity, 'I don't think it's a big enough case for him. He did pop in and take an interest, but I can't expect him to take it on.'

'You're insured?' asked Annie.

'Sore point at the moment,' said Felicity, 'I'm doing battle with the insurance company.'

'They're buggers,' said Annie.

'Yes, I'm having a bit of a struggle but James has offered to take them on.'

'I should let him,' said Annie, 'he'll probably do better than you.'

'Oh, thanks!' said Felicity.

'I'm not being rude,' said Annie, 'it's just because he's a fella, people always think they can take advantage of a woman, particularly a woman on her own. I should know, I've been alone long enough.'

'That sounds a bit bitter and twisted, Annie,' said Felicity.

Annie grinned at her, shifting slightly to make herself more comfortable. 'Just a fact. This boy is a lump, isn't he?'

'Would you like me to have him now?'

'No, don't disturb him, he's fine, he'll do, dear of him.'

While Felicity was enjoying the hospitality of Annie Trethewey, Keith was thundering down the motorway. Barbara had insisted that he should not see her off.

'It's pointless, Keith,' she said, 'stay the night and then leave bright and early to beat the traffic. I'll get the airport bus in, there is absolutely no point in you hanging about, I'd rather do it on my own anyway.'

After a struggle he had given in, had set the alarm for five and by five thirty was on his way west. His parting with Barbara had been friendly but oddly lacking in emotion and inevitably there had been a final jibe.

'Just you bear in mind, if you want to see something of your daughter, this is a journey we're going to have to make together in future.'

She was right, of course, and he supposed it was that which was depressing him. He had expected to feel a sense of liberation – no more set meals, no more recriminations, six weeks to do as he pleased – but instead he felt oddly deflated. He supposed it was because of their conversation the previous evening. She could not have spelled it out more clearly – he was a failure as a husband and a failure as a father and he believed she was probably right on both counts.

At Taunton services he stopped, got himself a coffee and a sandwich and rang Jack Curnow.

'Where are you?' Jack asked.

'Taunton,' Keith said.

'Blimey, that was quick, I thought you'd still be at Heathrow. Mrs Penrose's flight hasn't gone yet, has it?'

'No,' said Keith, 'but she wanted to do that bit on her own, so I left at the crack of dawn this morning. What's up?'

'Nothing more on Tanner's Cottage,' said Jack, 'but we've had another painting go, Penzance this time, one of those big Victorian houses up near the Bolitho School. The victim is an artist, his name is

Adam Mayfield, you may have seen his work, Maggie has. His house did not have an alarm, but he had a Picasso, would you believe.'

'We're not involved in this at the moment, are we?' Keith asked.

'No, no, it's not our case, it's just I thought you'd like to be kept informed in view of your friendship with Mrs Paradise.'

'Thank you, Jack,' said Keith, dismissively. The mention of Felicity should have brightened his mood but it had the reverse effect. He sat in the front of his car, drinking his coffee, staring morosely into space. He was tired, that was half the trouble – driving seven hundred miles in twenty-four hours would have been nothing for him even a few years ago. Now it felt like he'd done a day's work and it wasn't even nine o'clock. He would have to be very careful where Felicity was concerned. With Barbara away, the temptation to see her more often would be almost overwhelming. His mobile rang; he checked the screen. 'Miles, are you alright?'

'Not really,' Miles replied, 'well, yes really I suppose I am. The thing is, could you come and see me.'

'When?' Keith asked.

'It needs to be before one o'clock, I'm leaving at one o'clock.'

'Leaving? I thought you were at the Duchy for

another couple of weeks?'

'Something has come up,' Miles said, 'and I need to tell you about it.'

'Well, I'm in Taunton at the moment. One o'clock you say. I should be able to make it to you by about twelve, would that be OK?'

'Yes, you won't not come, will you?'

'That's a double negative, young man, and of course I'll be there.' Keith frowned as he put away his mobile and switched on the engine. Now what had happened to the boy?

The journey was fine until Keith reached Chiverton roundabout. The traffic moved at a snail's pace into the city as he headed towards the hospital. It was another gloomy day – cold, rainy and misty. A patch of mist had settled over the cathedral obscuring the main tower. Keith thought of Barbara in the air now, heading towards an Australian spring – it suddenly seemed rather an attractive proposition. It was just after 12.15 by the time he swung his car into the Duchy Hospital car park and hurried to Miles's room. Miles was still in bed, but the top half of him was dressed and there was a suitcase, Keith noticed, standing at the end of the bed.

'Sorry, sorry,' said Keith, 'the traffic was awful. What's up?' He sat down in the visitor's chair and studied Miles, who looked both pale and bewildered.

'You couldn't shut the door, could you?' Miles said, indicating the door to his room which Keith had left ajar. Keith got up and did as he was told. 'Hugo has defected so I'm going back up to be with Mother, she's arranged a home nurse.'

'What do you mean,' said Keith, 'Hugo's defected?'

Miles eyed him pityingly. 'Come on, Chief Inspector, brain in gear. Hugo, my so-called father, who is masquerading as my so called uncle, has gone over to the other side. He's gone to Russia. You know there was always talk of him being a double agent, well clearly he is, or rather was.'

'But why,' said Keith, 'why now? I don't understand it, and in any case I thought the Russians were after him, I thought that was why his poor brother was murdered.'

'I don't pretend to understand it either,' said Miles, 'he simply went. MI5 told my mother last night.'

Keith was truly shocked. 'You mean after all those years of marriage and shared children, he simply up and went without a word?'

Miles shrugged. 'Well, he was never the warmest of personalities, as you know, and I suppose in the circumstances, he didn't dare tell anybody.'

'Not even his wife?' Keith said.

'Nor his son,' said Miles.

'I am sorry,' said Keith. 'I was just so surprised by the news, I wasn't thinking about the impact it's having on you. How do you feel about it?'

'Relieved to be honest,' said Miles. 'I never liked the man, nor he me, but despite everything, I am very fond of my mother. I think we'll both have a better life now.'

'And he went of his own volition, he wasn't taken, abducted, I mean?' Keith asked.

'Apparently not.'

'The press are going to have a field day.'

Miles shook his head. 'No, no one is going to know. He is "Uncle Bob" after all. There is a cover story being worked out. Apparently my "uncle" wasn't enjoying life looking after me and my mother and so has gone back to doing whatever he was doing before. Presumably there's going to be a reason given as to why Uncle Bob has disappeared out of our lives. I don't know how they're handling it yet, but I don't see it as our problem,' said Miles shrugging his shoulders.

'Why in God's name did he do it?' Keith asked. 'Everyone thought he was his brother, he was safe, he was living in his own home with his wife and his son and absolutely no money worries.'

'Mother reckons he was bored,' said Miles. 'He

couldn't take a real active part in the business empire any more because he was supposed to be Uncle Bob who knew nothing about it. He also had to pretend his friends weren't really his friends. He had become something of a recluse with too much time on his hands.'

Keith shook his head. 'I just don't get it. I understand that the Russians were very successful in recruiting students from Cambridge, often young men who thought it was fashionable to be left-wing. However Hugo dragged himself from nothing to being a top industrialist, acquiring wealth and status along the way, and yet all the time believing in something that was totally alien to the life he had created. It is very odd.'

'He was a miner's son, remember,' said Miles. 'There has been an awful lot of bitterness surrounding the treatment of miners over the years, maybe that was what influenced him.'

'He never discussed politics with you?' Keith asked.

'He never discussed anything with me,' said Miles.

Keith stood up and began pacing up and down Miles's small room. 'What a mess,' he said, 'nothing is what it seems to be and old PC Plod here isn't even allowed to sort it out. What a world we live in; girls like your sister and Anya being abused and exploited and treated as worthless, then posers like Hugo Irving, one of the great and good, handing out largesse left, right and centre while he betrays his country. Half the world's children are starving to death; the West is living under a constant threat of terrorism, we're fighting a ridiculous war in Afghanistan that we can't win, we're all obsessed with consumerism, the acquisition of money and the next big shiny thing, we're running out of food and oxygen and the planet is heading towards boiling point...' Keith stopped in mid-stride. 'Sorry,' he said.

'It's OK, let me tell you a story,' said Miles. 'It may help.'

'Go on,' Keith encouraged him, calming down a little.

'When I was in Romania, when you came and found me, I visited my old orphanage. I told you that didn't I?' Keith nodded. 'I went twice, once on an official visit and then a second time. On the second occasion it was evening and I took with me a couple of packets of biscuits. There was a piece of scrubby grass outside the orphanage enclosed by a rusty old wrought iron fence. The grass was covered in dog faeces and there was the odd hypodermic needle lying about just to make it the ideal location for children to play in.' Keith had returned to his seat and was giving him all his attention now. 'I knew some of the older children were allowed to come out and play in the early evening. It was impossible to tell whether they were boys or girls, they all had their heads shaven, they were in raggedy clothes, they were very pale and listless. I sat on a bench in the garden and they played around me, it was difficult to tell their ages but they were between seven and ten I would think. There was about twenty of them. It was a beautiful evening, wonderful golden light, and somewhere at the top of the orphanage building above me, a woman was singing. She had a beautiful voice, truly operatic, I presumed she was singing to the children. I got out my biscuits and started handing them around. The children were very appreciative, they didn't snatch, they thanked me but they were clearly very hungry, they gobbled them up, they were so thin. There are no fat children in Romania.' Miles smiled at Keith. 'It was a moment of such extreme contrasts – the beautiful singing, the wonderful light, the wretched play area, the wretched children, the animated chatter amongst them because of the biscuits.'

'I can see that,' said Keith, quietly.

'I had just handed out the last biscuit, when to my horror, around the end of the building came another child. He or she was small and dirty and half-starved like the others. Seeing something was going on, the child ran over towards me. I held out my hands to show I had nothing, I felt awful, in despair. The child turned its attention from me to the recipient of the last biscuit. The two children faced one another, stood and stared at each other solemnly; then the child with the biscuit broke it in half and handed half to the new arrival. I have played that scene over in my head again and again,' said Miles, 'and it brings great comfort. You see, in that single gesture, of one starving child helping another, it makes me believe there is hope for the world.'

A nurse popped her head around the door. 'Miles, the ambulance is here, are you ready?'

'Yes,' said Miles. He glanced at Keith who was rather furtively blowing his nose.

'Sorry, it's children, they always get to me.' He wiped his eyes hurriedly.

'Will I ever see you again?' Miles asked.

'You come down to Cornwall often enough, don't you?'

'I suppose so,' said Miles, 'though after what's happened to Harry and Becky... I still have a lot of friends down here from when we had the house in St Ives, it's just that bad things seem to happen to me down here. I will come and see Anya though when I can travel. In the meantime, you couldn't come and see me, could you?'

'As it happens,' said Keith, 'I am going as far as Reading for Christmas but I have to be back in Truro the day after Boxing Day, in the evening anyway. I could pop up to London I suppose, there won't be much traffic about.'

'Come on Boxing Day,' Miles suggested.

'I can't really intrude on a family Christmas,' said Keith.

'Mother would like to talk to you, I'm sure, and as for the family Christmas, it's only going to be her and me. I'll confirm it once I've spoken to her.'

'Alright,' said Keith. The two men shook hands as a stretcher was wheeled into the room. Keith walked over to the door and stopped. 'I'll remember what happened in the orphanage garden, Miles, when life is getting me down. It's a good one.'

'I never got my grapes, Chief Inspector.'

'True,' said Keith, smiling and disappeared through the door.

9

Felicity spent a very pleasant evening in the Sloop with Tom Ward and Sarah. They had rung earlier in the day to say they had run out of her cards and could they come over and collect some more. Felicity had suggested they come to her cottage for a drink, but instead they had suggested the Sloop and what had begun as a drink had ended up with the three of them having supper. They were good company and belonged to a world outside West Cornwall, – a world to which Felicity herself had once belonged but from which she now felt increasingly remote – but it was interesting.

'The police came to see me today,' Tom said. 'There are some valuable paintings going missing from local homes and the police are going around to all gallery owners to make sure nobody tries to offload them. Why they bothered with me I don't know, they can see I only handle contemporary stuff. The sort of paintings they're talking about are way out of my league. I wonder who's behind it though? You wouldn't think there were many rich pickings down here, but by all accounts the villains seem to know what they're doing.'

Felicity saw no reason not to be honest. 'One of the victims was me.'

'What?' said Sarah.

'I have, or rather, had a little Constable, it belonged to my late mother-in-law, someone must have known it was there. They bashed my door in, took it off the wall and disappeared.'

'Felicity, that's awful,' said Tom, 'I'd no idea. I knew one of the burglaries was in St Ives because the police told me – St Ives, Carbis Bay and Penzance, I gather so far.'

'I didn't know about Penzance,' said Felicity, 'was that recently?'

'Yesterday, I think. I don't know why the police are messing around at local level, there is no way the paintings will still be in Cornwall, they're probably not even in the country by now.'

'You reckon?' said Sarah.

Tom nodded. 'The concept that any galleries around here would fence stolen paintings is a joke, I don't know what the police think they're up to.'

'Out of the country?' Felicity said, forlornly. 'That's awful, I can't bear it, the painting meant so much to my husband and his mother. I can't believe I've been such an idiot,' she sighed. 'I've been told a lot of stolen paintings do turn up again. Is that true, Tom?'

'Who told you that?' Tom asked.

'A policeman.'

'Wishful thinking, I would imagine, though I suppose he could be right. There have been some amazing cases haven't there, like the Mona Lisa? What you could think about doing when you get the insurance money is to buy something with it that you know your husband would have liked. What about that for an idea?'

'*If* I get the insurance money,' said Felicity, morosely.

In Truro Keith Penrose was feeling equally bleak. He had arrived home to an empty house. It was spotlessly clean and tidy – Barbara was nothing if not efficient – but it was just an empty shell. He found himself thinking about how it had been when the children were small, and how much he missed his old rescue greyhound, Buster. It just didn't feel right; he couldn't ever remember being in the house on his own for any length of time before. He searched in the freezer. Good as her word, Barbara had batch-cooked a number of meals for one. Keith looked at them in despair and then shut the freezer again. He put on the kettle, then turned it off; he opened the fridge, took out a bottle of wine, then put it back. 'Sod it,' he said aloud, picked up his jacket and headed out for the pub.

The following morning Keith had been in his office no more than five minutes when his phone rang. He had arrived at his desk early because there was no point in staying at home.

'Keith, it's Horace.'

'You're bright and early,' said Keith.

'Dedication to my work, old boy. I have some preliminary findings for you.'

'Go on,' said Keith.

'They're related, this chap in Manchester and our skeleton. It will be another couple of weeks before I can tell you precisely the nature of their relationship and then the odds will only be several hundred million to one.'

'That's good enough for me,' said Keith.

'In the meantime,' Horace said, 'they're definitely part of the same family tree. I thought it worth letting you know because it might be sufficient information for you to shake down whoever you feel might be responsible for the demise of our poor chap.'

'That's very good of you, Horace, how considerate.'

'As you know, I always aim to please,' said Horace, 'and I don't like the idea of some bastard getting away with murder for so long. He's been living the life of Riley for the last twenty-odd years while our victim has been fertilising the vegetable patch. Go get him, Chief Inspector.'

That's all very well, Keith thought, replacing the receiver, but his only real suspect was a sweet little old lady called Violet, well into her eighties. The thought of 'shaking her down', as Horace had so delicately put it, was not a pleasant thought and yet she had already lied to him once and it now looked as if the victim could be her husband. He opened the door to his office and shouted for Jack. 'Jack, you couldn't do a quick bit of research for me could you? Could you widen our search of the Symonds' family tree and see whether there is anybody other than David Symonds who could be the victim? It looks as though there is a DNA match although at the moment it's rather tenuous.'

'Done it, sir,' said Jack.

'You know sometimes Jack, you're not half bad – and the answer?'

'David Symonds was an only child, Violet has two sisters both older than her, both dead now, and as you know Andrew Symonds was also an only child. There is nobody in the immediate family who would have been the same sort of age as the body and David Symonds.'

'What about cousins? What about Violet's two

sisters, maybe they had sons?'

'I haven't checked that out sir, but I can do so.'
Jack eyed his boss shrewdly. 'You're just looking for
excuses not to go back to see Violet, aren't you?'

'She's lied already and you've obviously found
no evidence of an Australian connection as far as
David Symonds is concerned, have you?'

Jack shook his head. 'Absolute blank. Even in
1978 it wouldn't have been that easy to disappear
off the face of the earth.'

'If the body we've found is that of David
Symonds then it stands to reason that Violet
certainly knew who put him in the ground, even if
she didn't put him there herself.'

'She's a little woman, you said?' Jack asked.

Keith nodded. 'She is now, tiny in fact. Of
course people do shrink with age, but she could
never have been very big.'

'So she would have been hard-pressed to dig a
hole and put a big chap like her husband in the
ground without some help.'

'True,' said Keith. 'Just check out this cousin
thing for me, could you? Before I go frightening old
ladies, I need to be very sure of my facts.'

Keith sat alone in his car outside Violet's flat in
Bedford Road. He had driven to St Ives alone. It
was early evening and Jack needed to be home with

his young family. Keith by contrast had nothing to go home for. He sensed early evening might be quite a good time to talk to Violet. It was dark but lights were glowing inside Violet's flat. Maybe it would create an atmosphere of intimacy, maybe she would be more likely to open up to him. If she were younger he would have simply stormed in and demanded answers, but she was old, fragile and lonely. He heaved a great sigh; sometimes he loathed this job.

At last, unable to think of any further excuses as to why he should remain seated in his car, Keith clambered out wearily, walked up the steps to Violet's door and rang the bell. Time passed. Maybe she has gone to bed and I've left it too late he thought, but there seemed to be too many lights on to suggest she had already retired for the night. The cold dank day had turned into a cold dank night; there was a nasty little north-easterly blowing in from the sea. It was easy to imagine an old lady taking to her bed on such a night. Just when he was trying to decide whether to ring the bell again or abandon the whole project until the morning, the door was unlatched and Violet peered out.

'Oh there you are, come along in. I'm sorry it's taken me so long to get to the door, this weather makes me stiffer by the day.'

'I'm sorry to call so late,' Keith said.

'That's no problem dear, I'm not going anywhere on a night like this. Come along in.' She led him, not to the kitchen this time, but to a warm cosy sitting room. An electric fire with fake flames threw out a warm glow from a Victorian fireplace. Violet indicated a chair. 'Please sit down. Can I get you a glass of sherry?'

Keith shook his head. 'No thanks, not while I'm on duty, but why don't you sit down and I'll fetch one for you.' He spied a decanter and glasses at the far end of the room.

'Thank you,' she said and settled herself with a sigh of relief into a chair by the fire.

Keith returned with a glass of sherry and looked around for somewhere to sit. On the chair on the other side of the fire sat an enormous black and white cat.

'Push him off, do,' Violet said.

'I wouldn't dream of it,' Keith said, 'this is his home. I'll sit on the sofa.'

'That's kind of you,' said Violet, smiling at him.

This isn't going to be easy, Keith thought. 'Mrs Symonds, I won't mess around,' he said after a pause. 'We took a DNA sample from your son and the lab have already established it is some kind of match to the skeleton we found in Tanner's Cottage garden. It's too early to tell what the exact relationship is but there is a blood relationship and within about a week to ten days time we'll know exactly what that relationship is. Does that help you to help me identify who might have been buried in your garden?'

Violet was silent for several minutes. She took a sip of sherry and then with a shaking hand lowered the glass onto the little table beside her. She stared at Keith over the top of her half-moon glasses for a moment. 'You are a nice man,' she said, at last, 'and I think it would be a lot easier for you if I simply told you what happened, wouldn't it?'

'It certainly would,' said Keith. 'Just take your time.'

'My husband, David, was also a nice man when we first married. He had always liked a drop but after a year or two the drink started to take a hold on him. He'd do his work alright but then go straight from the farm to the pub and sometimes he wouldn't appear at home until closing time. It got so there was no point in even cooking him his tea.'

'Was Andrew born by then?' Keith asked.

Violet nodded. 'Yes, I think it was after the baby was born that he started drinking. I don't think he liked it that my time was so taken up with the baby.'

The temptation to ask questions was great but Keith kept quiet.

'When he was sober he wouldn't hurt a fly,' Violet said, 'but when he was drunk,' her voice faltered, 'when he was drunk…'

'He used to hit you?' Keith finished for her.

Violet nodded. 'I'd have the boy in bed, of course, before he got home and if he was late enough, I could be in bed and asleep too. Often he couldn't make it up the stairs when he got home but if he did…' Her face darkened, the misery of being an abused wife was suddenly very evident. 'I got better at avoiding trouble over the years, but I took a few knocks, a few broken ribs, teeth, a broken arm once – Social Services came around but I managed to persuade them I was just clumsy.'

'Why on earth did you stay with him?' Keith asked.

'I couldn't think what else to do. Unusually for those days, we owned that cottage. My parents died young and they left me and my sisters a little legacy. It was just enough for the deposit on a cottage. We owned it jointly, of course, with a joint mortgage and I just couldn't see how I could leave. To make matters worse, I didn't earn any money either, David didn't like me going out to work. I worked hard to eke out David's income, I kept chickens and I lied to you about the vegetable garden, it wasn't my husband's, it was mine, I grew all sorts in it. You're a Cornishman, I can see that, jobs in the seventies down here were few and far between, weren't they?'

Keith nodded. 'So what happened?' he asked gently.

She reached out, picked up her glass and took another sip of sherry. Keith waited patiently as she returned the glass to the table. It was a lengthy process. 'It was a summer's evening, August the 21st 1979,' she said at last in a faltering voice. 'Andy was sixteen, he and I were having a bit of supper outside in the garden. Andy had taken the plates into the kitchen to wash up while I enjoyed the last of the sunshine. He was a good boy. It was all so peaceful,' she said wistfully, 'and it was also the last time we had any peace. David came home unexpectedly early, he was in a towering rage. His boss at the farm had a friend who had apple orchards the other side of Hayle. I had just arranged to do some picking for him to raise a bit of extra cash, David had got it into his head that I was having an affair with him because I had been seen during the day talking to him. He came at me with his fists, called me a whore and a slut and started hitting me – worse than usual it was. I didn't see him coming – I was too busy trying to defend myself – but Andy ran up behind his father and cracked him over the head with the saucepan he had been washing. David went down like a stone. Andy said, "Come on

Mother let's get out of here before he comes round, he'll be in even more of a temper when he comes to." "We can't leave him like this," I said, but Andy was adamant that his father would be in even more of a rage because he'd have a headache as well as having the drink on him. I was all of a tremble but I did as Andy said. We left David where he was and walked out of the cottage, down the lane. We had only gone a few yards when a neighbour stopped us to pass the time of day. He was on his way to Marazion to pick his daughter up who was working at the Godolphin Arms. Andy suggested he gave us a lift and he did. For what seemed like hours, Andy and I walked about on the beach at Marazion. I bought us fish and chips and we sat on a rock. Andy wanted me to leave his dad, he said anything would be better than what I was going through. He also said he couldn't be there forever to protect me, he had to make a life for himself. We went round and round it. I believed, I still do, that if I tried to leave David he'd have killed me, maybe Andy too, I don't know. It wasn't really his fault though, dear, it was the drink.'

Keith nodded. It seemed incredibly poignant to hear Violet still defending her husband after all the years of abuse. 'So what happened next?' he asked.

'It was almost dark, there were no buses so we

started to walk home. After a while an empty taxi cab passed us, he had been dropping visitors in Marazion. The cab came from St Ives and the driver was the elder brother of a school friend of Andy's so he gave us a lift back into the village for a pound...' She hesitated. 'Now we get to the difficult bit.'

'Have another sip of your sherry,' Keith smiled at her, encouragingly.

She nodded and did as he suggested. 'When we arrived back at the house it was dark. I put on the lights in the kitchen, I remember that, and I also remember being surprised to see the back door was still open. I went out into the garden and there was David, still lying there. I must have screamed because Andy had gone straight up to the bedroom to see if his father was there and he came running down the stairs. We knelt down beside David and I stared at his face. He had his eyes wide open, I knew immediately that he was dead, but I touched his skin on his face, on his hands. He was cold, there was no life in him.

'The rest you've guessed,' Violet went on, after a long pause. 'We talked about contacting the police but Andy was just starting out on his life and neither of us could bear the thought of him going to prison. It was Andy's idea to bury him in the garden, but I agreed with him, I thought it was a good idea too. It was horrible. Andy dug the hole as deep as he could. I took off David's wedding ring, so that it wouldn't be too easy to identify him if he was ever found. I didn't know about DNA and all that in those days. It was about two o'clock in the morning by the time we put him in the ground. We covered him up, it was horrible, horrible, I can tell you.'

'I can imagine,' said Keith, 'but surely everybody must have asked what had happened to him?'

'Andy and I couldn't sleep, as you can imagine, so we talked about what we could possibly say. For a long time David had spoken about going to Australia, to a new life, being his own boss, getting away from me because I was a lazy, no-good wife. Every night in the pub he talked about it. So the next day I rang his boss and said David had run off with some woman to Australia. The news travelled around the village like wildfire. Everybody was very kind to me and to Andy and nobody queried it, because it was what everybody was expecting really. I thought the police would come and ask what had happened to him, to check you know, but nobody did. David's boss was very good to me, he found me work on the farm and Andy too, during holidays from college.'

'After having been through such a terrible experience together and shared this awful secret, I would have thought Andy and you would be very close?'

Violet shook her head. 'No, it's odd, isn't it dear? For a while we were, but after a bit I think the bad thing we had done became bigger than our relationship. It kind of loomed over us, eclipsed everything else. Every time we saw one another, we remembered what had happened. Andy is a bright boy, he wanted to be an architect and go into housing development. He said it couldn't fail as there weren't enough houses in this overcrowded little island of ours, and he's proved to be right. He applied for a place at Manchester University and he's rarely been home since. I don't blame him.'

'So why did you tell me he died in a motorcycle accident?'

Violet met Keith's eye, it was hard to believe she was lying now. 'Stupid of me, wasn't it? I thought that if maybe I pretended I hadn't got a son, you'd leave things be, that you wouldn't go looking for him. I should have known in these days of computers and the like, it wouldn't work. It is true though, we don't see each other much. I can't stand his wife – stuck-up bitch – has no time for me. In a way it suits us both, me and Andy, I think it's better we're apart.'

'Tell me Mrs Symonds, when you came back to the house after you'd walked and talked at

Marazion, was your husband in exactly the same position as he was when you had left him?'

Violet shook her head. 'No that was the awful part, the tables and chairs in the garden were all turned upside down, I think he had tried to stand up. He was very, very drunk you see, as well as having a bash on the head and he must have tried to get up and then dropped down dead, I assume.'

'Was there much blood?' Keith asked.

'A bit, we didn't see it until the next morning. Andy hadn't realised he'd hit his dad so hard as to draw blood, there was just a little on the grass, we washed it off with a hose.'

'And Andy was with you from the moment you left the house after he hit his father, until you both came back and found the body?'

Violet nodded. Her eyes were full of tears now and she was shaking. She reached for a handkerchief from inside her cardigan sleeve and dabbed her eyes. 'Are you going to arrest me now?' she asked Keith in a tremulous voice.

'No,' said Keith.

'What about Andy?' she faltered.

'No, not him either.' It was breaking all the rules to tell a suspect details of a case, but he couldn't leave things as they were. This poor old woman and her son had carried guilt with them for over twenty years, it was time he helped them lay down their burden. Keith stood up and walked over to Violet's chair, crouching down beside her so that his face was level with hers. 'Violet,' he said, 'Andy didn't kill your husband, someone shot him.'

Violet stared at Keith. 'I don't think so, dear.'

'Yes,' said Keith. 'We found a bullet. Our forensic team think he was probably shot through his heart. We found he had a slight fracture to the skull, which was probably caused by Andy and the saucepan, but our pathologist doesn't think the blow was hard enough to have left him unconscious for more than a few minutes. Andy didn't kill your husband, Violet, but the question is, who did?'

She began to cry in earnest then, her hands over her face. Keith produced a large white handkerchief and she took it gratefully and began to sob.

'All these years,' she said.

Keith took her sherry glass and refilled it, then he returned to the sofa and waited.

'I must talk to Andy,' she said at last.

Keith nodded. 'Yes, but it doesn't end here. What you and Andy need to do now to help me is to think who hated your husband enough to have shot him. The bullet was from a hunting rifle, a countryman who took his sport seriously.'

Violet stared at Keith wild-eyed. 'Pretty much everybody hated David.'

'When you've got over the shock of all this,' Keith said, 'you need to talk to Andy and see if either of you can come up with any names that might help us.'

'Aren't you really going to charge me with anything?' Violet asked, tremulously.

'Not at the moment,' said Keith, 'but I'm going to have to talk it all through with my boss and I can't promise anything at this stage. There is a lesson here though, which shows that taking the law into your own hands doesn't work. If you had reported your husband's death to the police, we would have established he had been shot almost immediately, instead of which you and your son have carried the guilt with you…'

'Stop,' said Violet, 'I don't even want to think about it.'

'Sorry,' said Keith, 'I didn't mean to lecture you.'

'We were so afraid of him, you see,' Violet said, 'we couldn't think straight.'

'It's alright,' said Keith, 'I understand, I truly do.'

10

The temptation was just too great; the conversation with Violet had depressed him. All those wasted years believing that her son had killed her husband and all the years wasted before that, in accepting abuse because she could think of nothing else to do. What was it that made some people victims? She was clearly an intelligent woman and must have been very pretty in her day. There was a natural kindness to her; she'd have made a good wife to any man, so why did she choose that one? Keith remembered in his early days at the Met, his immediate boss saying to him 'Our job, son, is to enforce the law, but never, ever to sit in judgement – not on the villains nor on the victims. Unless you've lived that person's life, unless you know intimately what's happened to them during the course of it, you have no right to judge them.' It was easy to say any normal woman would have run away from the abuse, but what did he really know of Violet Symonds – nothing, and did he believe he now had the truth? – he was still not sure.

He left his car in Bedford Road, walked down Fore Street and then turned left up to Jericho Cottage. It wasn't so much a decision, it just happened. He stood in front of the newly-repaired and repainted purple front door. He hesitated and then pressed the bell. After a pause the door was opened. She was wearing an ancient T-shirt, some tracksuit bottoms, her hair was wet from the shower and she was wearing not a scrap of make-up. Keith thought she looked magnificent.

'Keith,' she said, 'what on earth are you doing here?'

'Back to Bedford Road again, I'm afraid.'

'You look exhausted. What's up?'

He shrugged. 'Can I come in for a few minutes? I won't stay, I promise.'

'You certainly can, provided you let me tidy myself up. Go upstairs and open a bottle of wine – there's some white in the fridge or some red through in the sitting room – I don't mind which.'

He knew she preferred white so he delved around in the fridge and then searched for some glasses and a corkscrew. Within minutes Felicity reappeared. The T-shirt had been replaced by a mad pink fluffy sweater, the tracksuit bottoms remained, her feet were still bare, but her hair was brushed – she still looked magnificent. He poured the wine.

'You'd rather have red,' she said, accusingly.

'No I wouldn't,' he protested.

'You're a liar,' she said, 'which is a very bad trait to find in a policeman but thank you for opening white on my account.' They smiled at one another and clinked glasses. 'I can't bear going into the sitting room at the moment, do you mind just sitting around the Aga?'

'My favourite place,' he said and lowered himself into a Windsor chair.

'So, why so glum?' she asked.

He shrugged. 'I don't know, difficult case.'

'Do you want to talk about it?'

'I shouldn't really, but I always say that and then I always end up telling you about it.'

'Go on then,' said Felicity, smiling.

Keith told her everything; Violet's initial reaction, the discovery of her son and finally of his meeting that evening. When he had finished he stood up and refilled both their glasses.

'Do you believe her?' Felicity asked.

Keith nodded. 'I think so, but something still niggles – what, I don't know. What I do know is that I desperately want to believe her.'

'So, she buried her husband but she didn't kill him. Is that an offence, I presume it is?'

Keith nodded. 'Yes, yes of course it is but given her age and the circumstances I don't think she will go to prison, particularly if we can find the real killer.'

'And the boy, Andy, he was with his mother the whole time?'

Keith nodded appreciatively. 'Yes, that was my initial thought too, that the son had somehow contrived to come back and finish off his father while he was still unconscious. However from the moment they left the house until the moment they got back they were together the whole time, according to Violet.'

'But you're dealing with a mother,' said Felicity, 'I don't think you can automatically assume that she has told you the truth about that. I'd lie through my teeth to protect my children. I'm a pacifist but I could easily kill someone if they hurt one of my children or grandchildren.'

'Me too,' said Keith, and they smiled at each other. 'So you're saying that Violet possibly knew her husband had been shot and suspected it was her son?'

'I'm not saying that at all,' said Felicity, 'I'm just saying that protecting her son will be her top priority. You were there, you interviewed her, what do you think?'

'She appeared totally astonished by the fact we have found that her husband could not have died from his head injury and that he appears to have been shot through the heart or close enough to kill him. Like you, though, I think she's more than capable of lying to cover for her son. She's already done that by trying to make us believe that he was dead. Somehow, though, I also believe that whoever shot David Symonds was neither his wife nor his son.'

'So, that being the case,' said Felicity, 'you just have to find the chap who pulled the trigger.'

'I like the use of the word "just" making it sound simple to uncover what happened in a murder which took place over thirty years ago.'

'Where do you start with something like that?'

'I need to talk to Violet again and we need to talk to Andy, to see if his father had any specific enemies, that's the starting point. I am hoping both of them will be very anxious to be helpful. Now we know what really happened, they'll be wanting to clear their names – so they're the most likely source of information.'

'But how do you prove it, how do you turn a suspicion into a prosecution?'

'God knows,' said Keith, smiling. 'Look, let's change the subject. Tell me, how are you getting on with the stolen painting – are the insurance company being helpful yet?'

'No,' said Felicity, 'we're in a state of hiatus. Tom was saying he can't see any point of the police searching in this area, the painting will be long gone, a painting that important.'

'Tom?' Keith asked, trying to ignore a twinge of jealousy.

'Tom Ward, he runs the Windward Gallery over in Penzance. He's buying a lot of my paintings at the moment and I was talking to him and his girlfriend in the pub the other night. They reckon my poor little painting probably isn't even in the country and certainly not in Cornwall. Apparently the police have been going round the galleries like his, but it all seems pretty pointless.'

'He's probably right,' said Keith. 'So are your paintings selling well?'

'Certainly they are – through Tom at least, I'm selling masses. It's such a help, I'm always so tight financially.'

'Are you?' said Keith. 'Sorry, I don't mean to pry but you had such a big house in Oxford, I've always imagined you had no major money problems.'

'I didn't like where Charlie's money had come from,' Felicity said. 'I sold the house, bought this cottage, kept back a few thousand pounds in order to renovate it, bought myself a new car and gave the rest to a drug rehabilitation centre.'

'That was a magnificent gesture,' said Keith.

'Charlie's legacy felt like blood money. I didn't

want it, it wouldn't have felt right. It was a relief actually, to give it away. I wasn't being noble.'

'Where money is concerned, a lot of people seem to be able to overcome their scruples,' Keith said.

That may be true,' Felicity admitted. 'Anyway the result is, apart from the clothes I stand up in, this cottage, my car and of course Harvey, my assets are few and even fewer now the painting has gone. I live very simply but it suits me.'

'It certainly does,' said Keith, shifting awkwardly in his chair. 'Look, I'd better get going.'

'I have some fresh pasta in the fridge, why don't I knock us up a bowl? It'll take no more than a few minutes – that and a quick coffee and it won't matter that you've had a couple of glasses of wine.'

'Are you sure?' Keith began.

'Of course I'm sure. Budge over, I can't get at the Aga.'

He sat back comfortably in the chair watching her deft movements as she prepared pasta and a salad and grated some fresh parmesan. There seemed to be no need to talk. He felt at ease, content, the day's trials began slipping away. She turned to him and smiled, a radiant smile that seemed to light up his world.

'It's ready. What would you like to drink?'

'Better be water,' he said. She filled an

earthenware jug and put it on the table. He sat down. 'This is very good of you,' he said.

'Don't be ridiculous, it's nothing. Thinking about it, this is the first time I've ever cooked – if you can call it cooking – anything for you. You are always taking me out to lunch, so it's about time I reciprocated, even in such a meagre fashion.'

'It's very welcome,' Keith said. They ate their pasta in silence for a moment. 'I find eating alone, since Barbara left for Australia rather dull.' Keith said.

'How long will she be away?'

'For about six or eight weeks.'

'Goodness,' said Felicity, 'what are you doing about Christmas?'

'I'm going up to my sister, she lives near Reading. I'm on duty over New Year anyway, so it will just be a couple of days – Christmas Day and Boxing Day – and then I'll be back.'

'That'll be strange for you. When did you last have Christmas away from your home?' Felicity asked.

Keith put down his spoon and fork. 'I've missed Christmases of course – sometimes I've been on duty; sometimes I've been on call and something has gone wrong; sometimes there's been something serious to deal with. Mostly, though, I've been around and, of course, always based at home. You're right, it will be strange.'

'You should have gone with her.'

'Don't you start,' he said, with a smile.

'It would have done you good, going out there and seeing Carly. I'm only saying all this because you seem a little sad.'

'I'm not sad for me,' said Keith, 'I'm just sad about Violet Symonds, sad about all the people who put up with abuse when they don't really need to do so. If only they realised there was a way out. It's a funny old business, police work: you see the best and you see the worst of humanity. More often the worst of course, but a pattern develops – we're not as individual as we think we are, our human frailty is so predictable. Sorry,' he said, 'I'm being very boring. Miles has gone back up to London – there's something different to talk about.'

'Why?' said Felicity.

Keith wanted so much to tell her but he knew it was a betrayal of confidence which was totally unacceptable. 'His treatment is going well and he thought he could go home. He's going to come back down to visit Anya though, when he's better. I'm not saying romance is in the air, that's going too far, but I think a friendship is blossoming and I think it's a very positive one – for both of them.'

'I'm sure it is,' said Felicity, 'I'm so pleased. Would you like some coffee?'

Keith shook his head. 'No, I'd better get going. It's been a long day and I need an early start in the morning. Besides…' He hesitated.

'Besides what?' Felicity asked.

He shook his head. 'Nothing. Can I help with the washing up?'

'You certainly can't, Chief Inspector.' She saw him downstairs, out onto the street and waved him off until he was out of sight. He had made no attempt to touch her, kiss her, anything – she knew exactly why.

11

'Is that Andrew Symonds?'

'It is.'

'This is Chief Inspector Keith Penrose of Devon and Cornwall Constabulary.'

'Now what?' Andrew Symonds said, ungraciously.

'I need to interview you, sir.'

'I've been interviewed, I've given a DNA sample, that's an end to it.'

'I'm afraid it isn't, sir,' Keith said. 'Firstly, we have established that the skeleton at Tanner's Cottage is a relation of yours and secondly your mother has told me the full story of how you buried your father, believing you had killed him.'

'What a load of absolute rubbish. How dare you intimidate an old woman! She doesn't know what she's talking about, you've confused her.'

'She knows exactly what she's talking about,' said Keith. 'I'm a busy man, as I'm sure you are too, Mr Symonds. We can do this the easy way or the difficult way – the easy way would be for you to come down to St Ives so that I can talk to you and your mother together to see if we can at least come up with a theory as to who might have killed your father.'

'I don't know what you mean.' For the first time the veneer of anger and aggression had slipped.

'I'll tell you what I mean when we meet,' said Keith, his voice steely.

'I can't get away at the moment.'

'Fine,' said Keith, 'then we'll do it the difficult way which means that I'll send a squad car around to your office within the next half hour, you'll be taken into custody and held there until I can find the time to come up to Manchester to interview you. It might be several days before an opportunity presents itself.'

'And what possible grounds do you have for arresting me?'

'Because you're refusing to give information concerning the very serious crime of murder.' There was a silence between them. 'Look,' said Keith, 'I don't presume to know why you and your mother have fallen out, but I get the feeling from her that it concerns the fact that you have been carrying this joint guilt and the very sight of each other reminds you of what you have done. You committed a crime,

Mr Symonds, by burying your father in the garden but you didn't kill him, someone else did that and we have to find out who. When we do, I think it will give both you and your mother some peace of mind. I can talk to her some more and will do so, but two heads are better than one and I think she needs your support right now. Either way I will talk to you in the immediate future and it's up to you as to how and where I do it.'

'I'll drive down tonight,' said Andrew Symonds, still giving nothing away. 'What's the name of that hotel up on the hill above St Ives?'

'Tregenna Castle,' said Keith.

'Right, I'll book myself in there. Tell mother I'm on my way.'

'No,' said Keith, 'I'm not a messenger boy, *you* tell your mother you're on your way. Given your long drive I suggest we meet at your mother's cottage at eleven o'clock tomorrow morning.'

Keith had just finished the call when Jack Curnow came into his office.

'He's a nasty piece of work,' said Keith.

'Who?' Jack asked.

'Andrew Symonds. I've told him to come down here so I can discuss everything with him and his mother and he's not a happy chap.'

'Is there anything more you want me to do regarding the case?' Jack asked.

'I think the only thing you can do is to ask around some of the older folk in the village.'

'As I told you, there's precious few left,' Jack said.

'Well, scratch about a bit, see what you can find, we're looking at old scores to be settled, that sort of thing. It could well be that the man – and I presume it was a man – with a hunting rifle who killed David Symonds is long dead but I need to know who it is. The only way I can see a judge is going to take a lenient view of what Violet Symonds did, is if I can provide him with a killer.'

'And what about Andrew?' Jack asked.

'He was a minor, but it was his mother's job to report what had happened. But after years of abuse she panicked and she is now a very old woman. We need to know who killed David Symonds to really make sure she's not threatened with prison.'

The day dragged by for Keith. He kept wondering how Miles was getting on with his mother back in London, he wondered what Violet Symonds was feeling, whether she regretted telling him what had happened, and above all, he wondered about Felicity. He had left just in time the previous evening before he made a fool of himself. He hadn't wanted to go, he had felt so comfortable, so at home. The day dragged on. Around midday,

Barbara rang, still locked into UK time and wide awake although it was the middle of the night in Australia.

'This is a wonderful place Keith, you must come here soon, you'd love it.'

'Would I?' Keith asked. 'I'm so glad you're having a good time.'

'Carly and Graham have this fantastic little house, almost on the beach, in a suburb of Sydney called Balmoral. I'm staying there too, there is plenty of room. We're going to the opera tomorrow night. Everything is wonderful, it's all so relaxed and the weather is marvellous. Carly looks great.'

'Can I talk to her?'

'No, of course you can't silly, she's fast asleep as is every other sensible person in Australia, except me. Are you managing?'

'I'm fine,' said Keith. 'Send my love to Carly.'

It was just after five when Keith was contemplating, without relish, an evening at home alone that Jack burst through his door.

'We've got a fatality, sir, just up the road at the top end of Lemon Street. It looks like a murder and a robbery.'

'Any details?' Keith asked.

'Not much, the victim has broken his neck falling off an outside staircase apparently, but not before being coshed over the head. There is some talk of a painting going missing, I don't know if it could be the same…'

'Let's go,' said Keith.

'Neil Mavers is on it,' said Jack, referring to Detective Inspector Neil Mavers, for whom Keith had little regard.

'He won't mind us joining in,' said Keith, knowing this not to be true.

Detective Inspector Neil Mavers was a big bloke by anybody's estimation. If you were casting him in a film, he'd be a villain not a policeman. He had played county rugby in his youth, as a prop, and still had the look about him – the broken nose, the thick short neck and one spectacular cauliflower ear – but he'd gone to seed, his paunch being the biggest thing about him these days. Keith did not approve of this; he thought it was a copper's duty to stay fit. The man was only in his mid-forties, he'd be dead by sixty if he wasn't careful. Keith and Jack ducked under the tape which cordoned off the pavement outside the house in Lemon Street. It was an elegant terraced house, of the Queen Anne period. An ambulance was parked on the pavement. In front of it Keith recognised Horace Greenaway's car.

'Keith.' Neil Mavers extracted himself from a group of officers gathered on the pavement. The two men shook hands. 'What brings you here?' Neil asked. 'Come to see the show, we don't often have a murder in Truro, do we?'

Keith hated this sort of talk, the disrespect to the victim.

'I'm here because I think it might be linked to another couple of cases, well three actually, over St Ives way.'

'Really? I haven't heard of any major incidents over there.'

'Art theft,' said Keith. 'I gather a painting has been taken.'

'It would appear so,' said Neil. 'The main thing is a man has been killed.'

'He disturbed the burglary?' Keith asked.

Neil nodded. 'It looks like it,' he conceded, 'it appears the villain or villains came in the front door, as you can see.'

Jack had already detached himself from the group and was examining the front door.

'Don't touch anything,' Neil shouted at him, unnecessarily.

Jack raised his head and met his boss's eye, one eyebrow slightly raised. 'This looks very familiar, sir,' he said.

'Do you mind if I take a look inside?' said Keith. 'I see Horace is here.'

'Be my guest,' said Neil Mavers, with a false

smile.

It was a beautiful house. An elegant sweep of staircase took Keith and Jack up to the first floor from which they entered through double doors into a large drawing room. Keith, no expert, cast his eye around the room and was impressed. He noticed the porcelain figurines above the fireplace, the antique furniture, the paintings – except the one blank square where a single painting had been removed. There were thousands of pounds tied up in this room but the villain had gone for just the one painting; he clearly knew what he was doing. At the far end of the drawing room were French windows which stood open, allowing a chilly breeze to invade the elegant room. Keith walked over to them and through the doors, which in turn led onto a small balcony and from the balcony a wrought-iron staircase spiralled down into the garden below. Search lights had been set up in the garden and Keith could make out the figure of Horace Greenaway kneeling over the body of a man. He hurried down the staircase.

'What have we got there, Horace?' he asked, joining the small group which included two paramedics obviously preparing to take the body away.

'Ah, Keith, I didn't think this was your case?'

'It's not,' said Keith, 'but I think it might be linked to some other art thefts, so I've tagged along.'

'I can't be exactly sure of the sequence of events. Horace nodded at the paramedics. 'You can take him away now.' He stood up and brushed himself down and walked a few yards away, indicating Keith to follow him. He pointed up to the balcony above. 'I imagine when the thief or thieves broke down the door, they assumed the house was empty. In fact, this poor fellow,' he said, indicating towards the body, 'was in the garden. Maybe the noise of the door being staved in brought him inside, or simply that he was on his way back into the house in any event. Either way, he must have reached the balcony just as the picture was being taken. He was struck on the head but he was facing his assailant so they caught him on the right temple. It was a really vicious blow, hard enough maybe for him to have reeled back and fallen over the balcony. Alternatively, he may have been pushed. The result is a broken neck – dreadful shame, nice fellow.'

'You knew him?' Keith asked.

'Not well, he's a friend of some friends of mine. His name is Christopher Drummond, he's a retired Cambridge don, frightfully bright. His wife tragically died of cancer a few years ago and he decided to make a fresh start down here in Truro. His daughter works at the hospital, she's a gynaecologist, married to a farmer, they live out Stithians way. She is going to be devastated, she's an only child and she and her father were very close.'

'What's her name?' Keith asked.

'Emma,' said Horace, 'Emma Dakin, but at work she has kept her maiden name, she's known as Emma Drummond in the hospital.'

Keith frowned at his old friend. 'You're being unusually helpful, Horace.'

'Just giving you a head start over that idiot, Mavers. Can't stand the man, he's even more of a pain in the backside than you are, Penrose, and that's saying something. Besides, I obviously won't be doing the autopsy myself, as I knew Christopher, so I don't know whether Mavers will patch you in as things develop. Actually, I thought I might go and see whether he would let me break the news to Emma. He has the sensitivities of a charging rhino, I can't imagine he'd be much good at it.'

'You really aren't very fond of Neil Mavers, are you?' Keith said, with a smile.

Horace merely grunted in response. 'If you are able to let me have some more details of the case ,' Keith said, as they climbed the staircase. 'There's been three thefts of art in the area in the last few weeks; one in Carbis Bay, one in Penzance and Felicity Paradise had a Constable taken from her cottage in St Ives.'

'Aah, the fair Felicity,' said Horace, 'how is she?'

'She's in good spirits,' said Keith, keeping his voice very neutral. 'I haven't seen much of her in the last year, but she seems fine.'

'So she's kept out of trouble for once, most unusual. I like that woman, lots of spirit and a damn good looker for her age.' Keith decided the best thing he could do was to say nothing. 'You'd better tell her about this before it's all over the media. The newshounds are already on the street, so I noticed when I came in.'

'Why,' asked Keith, 'does she know Christopher Drummond as well?'

'No, no, dear boy, just try using your imagination for once. She's a woman living alone, she hears on television or reads in the newspaper that this is likely to be another art theft in similar modus operandi to the stealing of her own painting – only this time someone winds up dead. Very upsetting for a woman, thinking a potential murderer had been in her house. Honestly Keith, you policemen – you're completely devoid of any sensibilities. Talking of which, where is Mavers?'

It was just before seven when Keith reached home. He poured himself a glass of wine and listened to *The Archers* while he cooked a shepherd's pie from the freezer and made a salad from some rather suspect ingredients in the bottom of the fridge. He munched his way through the solitary meal, his mind flicking between the two cases which were absorbing his thoughts at the moment. The meeting with Violet and her son – he had no idea how that would go. Then these art thefts – clearly whoever was taking the paintings was an expert. They knew exactly what they were looking for, they were not diverted by anything else even in a house so fine as Christopher Drummond's. They were completely single-minded, stealing to order which was why there was no subtlety in their mode of entry. They simply beat the door down, went in, took what they wanted and left. Only this time it had gone tragically wrong. If Christopher Drummond had just stayed in his garden he would be alive now. Life's frailty, and the evidence of it, never failed to unsettle Keith. He finished his meal, washed his plate and then picked up his mobile from the kitchen table.

'It's me,' he said into the receiver.

'I know that,' Felicity replied, 'your name has just flashed before my eyes. Are you feeling better today?'

'Yes, thanks for the meal last night.'

'Actually I was going to ring you, there's a vague pattern emerging around these art thefts.'

'Before you start on that,' Keith said, 'there is something I need to tell you.'

'Oh no, bad news?' Felicity said, instantly picking up on the tone of his voice.

'Well, sort of,' Keith said, 'there's been another art theft, this time in Truro, today, in Lemon Street. The pattern was identical, door broken down, single painting taken, the difference is that someone died.'

'What do you mean,' said Felicity, 'someone died?'

'The man whose painting was stolen, he surprised the villains and they coshed him. Then he either fell or was pushed over the balcony and broke his neck.'

'God, how awful,' said Felicity.

'Only, I thought I'd better tell you before you heard anything about it. I didn't want you worrying about the fact that the same person had obviously been in your house. This villain is not a natural killer. He may not have even pushed Drummond over the balcony, he may have just fallen over. In any case, he would never come back to your house, he got what he came for.'

'This is all extremely kind of you, Chief

Inspector,' Felicity said, 'and very thoughtful. It would have been a bit of a shock if I'd just read about it out of the blue.'

Keith thought for a moment about admitting the idea had been Horace's and then decided to bask in the reflected glory. 'Anyway, all I'm really trying to say is don't let it worry you. The media will do their gory best no doubt to frighten us all.'

'Thanks, message received and understood. Poor chap though, I'm most relieved that Harvey and I didn't disturb our thief.'

'So you were going to ring me?' Keith asked.

'Oh yes,' said Felicity. 'Now and again I dip into a life class at the St Ives School of Art, it helps keep my work slightly more disciplined, I find. Anyway, I went this morning and I met a woman there I had never seen there before. Her name is Jan Shankland. We got talking and it turns out she is the person from whom the painting was taken in Carbis Bay. She's a local painter, I don't know if you've seen her work?'

'Not knowingly,' said Keith. 'Is she any good?'

'I think her work is ghastly, very crude, but it sells a lot better than mine, I suspect.'

'False modesty, Mrs Paradise, it doesn't suit you.'

'Anyway,' said Felicity, ignoring him, 'the interesting bit is that the other theft over in

Penzance was from Adam Mayfield, now you must know him?'

'You mean Adam Mayfield the artist, yes I know about that.'

'Yes, of course I mean Adam Mayfield the artist,' said Felicity. 'So you see the connection, don't you?'

'Not really,' said Keith.

'Keith, for heaven's sake concentrate – we're all local artists. Adam is way out of my league, and Jan's, but we're all people who paint and sell our paintings locally and we've all had a valuable painting stolen. There has to be a connection.'

'Isn't it simply that all three of you are artists and therefore love art? I appreciate that there are people who collect art because it's a sound investment, but most people who invest in a beautiful painting do so because they love art and artists love art, like writers love books and musicians love music.'

'I think you're being very obtuse, Chief Inspector, you're not concentrating or even attempting to take me seriously. Still, no change there, I suppose.'

'Now, now,' said Keith. 'I hear what you say, but I have to admit I don't really think it's relevant.'

'Then do me a favour,' said Felicity, 'this poor chap Christopher Drummond, find out if he is an artist and if he is, or rather was, you'll have to take me seriously.'

'I always take you seriously,' Keith said.

12

Keith and Jack arrived twenty minutes early for the appointment in Bedford Road with Violet Symonds and her son, Andrew. The traffic had been extremely light.

'I can't believe it's less than three weeks to Christmas,' said Jack, as he parked the car. 'What are you doing for Christmas, sir?'

'I'm going to my sister's, she lives just outside Reading. I thought I'd go up on Christmas Eve and come back the day after Boxing Day.'

'It's a long way for so short a trip.'

'Not really,' said Keith, 'you know what they say about visitors – like fish they go off after three days. She'll have had more than enough of me by then.'

'Are you close?' Jack said. 'If you don't mind me asking.'

'I suppose we are,' said Keith, 'we're very fond of each other. We spent our childhood together, we're only twenty-two months apart in age. It's just you know how life is these days – families all split up, living at opposite ends of the country and barely seeing one other. I've been a rotten brother really, rotten husband, rotten father too, apparently.'

Jack looked embarrassed. 'Sorry sir, I don't know how to respond to that. I'm sure you're not.'

'I'm sorry,' said Keith, 'it comes from too much introspection being on my own – it's not good for a person.'

'You ought to come around and see us, Maggie would love to have you for supper.'

'I'd like that too,' said Keith, 'now shall we go?'

'It's only ten-fifty, sir.'

'I suspect they'll be waiting for us though,' Keith said. 'Let's do it.'

He was right. Violet answered the door almost immediately.

'Come in dear,' she said, and led him straight into the sitting room, Jack following. Introductions were made all round. Andrew Symonds was a tall man, tall and dark with strong angular features. At first glance there was nothing of his mother in him, then Keith spotted a slight cleft in his chin, just as Violet had. Otherwise he had to be his father's son which, Keith speculated, must be quite hard for both of them in the circumstances.

'I'll fetch you some coffee,' Violet began.

'Don't worry Mrs Symonds,' said Keith, 'there

are too many of us today. We had some coffee, Jack and I, before we left the station.'

Violet stood poised as if for flight, then with obvious reluctance, she sat down in a chair on the opposite side of the room from her son. Keith wondered how they were getting on.

'Right,' he said, 'I don't really need to tell anyone why we're here but I will just recap. I'm not recording anything today although we will need you both to make formal statements. However, I am asking Jack here to make notes. Please recognise that this is simply an informal chat with a view to trying to resolve the matter. My job is to find out the truth of what happened on that summer's evening in 1979, but it is not my job to criticise, to accuse or to point the fingers of blame, we just need to find out what happened.' He cleared his throat. 'On the 21st of August, as I understand it, Mrs Symonds, your husband David came home early. He was drunk and abusive, neither of which was unusual. You were in the garden having just finished supper with your sixteen-year-old son, Andrew. Your husband started beating you and Andrew, in an attempt to save you, hit your husband over the head with a saucepan probably the edge of the saucepan I would think, having discussed matters with the pathologist. Your husband fell to the ground unconscious. You then both left the premises. Why was that?'

'It was my idea,' said Andrew, speaking for the first time, 'I knew when he came round it wouldn't just be Mum he would be after, he'd be after me too. I had never hit him before, but I was frightened, frightened for both of us.'

Violet gave him a look of gratitude; perhaps love was going too far, but there was evidence of warmth and emotion.

'I can understand that,' said Keith. 'So you left the house and had you any idea where you were going at that stage?'

Both of them shook their heads. 'We just wanted to get out,' Violet said.

'And then you met a neighbour who was going to Marazion?'

'Yes.'

'Can you tell me the name of that neighbour?'

'Yes, yes his name was Frank Edwards, he's been long dead now though. He was an old boy even then,' said Violet. She seemed a little calmer now.

'That's okay, Jack has just made a note of it for the record. He drove you to Marazion and dropped you off and you then walked and talked on the beach and had fish and chips. What did you talk about?'

Both mother and son frowned. They frowned

in the same way, a single line between their eyes. Keith found it oddly touching.

'We didn't talk much about David,' Violet said at last, 'did we, dear?' She looked enquiringly at her son.

'I think we mainly discussed what I was going to do about my future,' Andrew volunteered.

'You're an architect, I understand,' said Keith.

'Yes, it's a long training, we hadn't much money...' He hesitated.

'Go on,' said Keith.

'And we realised it wasn't going to be possible for me to train as an architect so we were trying to work out what else I could do.'

'But you did become an architect?' Andrew nodded. 'We'll come back to that later. So when you'd finished your fish and chips you realised you had to go home?'

'We hadn't any money left,' Violet said. 'We didn't know what to do.'

'There wasn't a friend or neighbour you could have asked to help?'

'I didn't like people knowing our business, I didn't want people to know that David hit me.'

'I understand,' said Keith, 'so you started to walk, a fair way from Marazion to St Ives and it was dark now?'

'No, getting dusk,' said Andrew.

'We'd not long got out of Marazion when this taxi passed us, it belonged to the elder brother of a friend of Andrew's,' said Violet.

'Can you tell me the name?' Keith asked.

Violet shook her head. 'I don't know, I can't remember. Andy?'

Andrew thought for a moment. 'I think his name was Ian, I know his younger brother was called George.'

'Surname?' Jack asked.

'Jennings, Ian Jennings I think,' said Andrew.

'And he would have been quite a young chap?'

'Oh yes, in his early twenties I would think.'

'So there is a good chance we could track him down to verify the story?'

'If he remembers,' said Andrew, 'it was a long time ago. It was a momentous day for us, mother and I, we'll never forget it, but for anyone else… he just helped out a couple on his way home from a fare.'

'I take the point,' said Keith, 'still we can try. So this Ian Jennings dropped you off in the village?'

'Yes, almost outside our front door,' said Violet.

'You went into the house and there you found the body of your husband still in the garden.'

Neither of them spoke for a moment, then Andrew cleared his throat, he shifted in his chair. 'We went into the kitchen together and I put on the kettle. I said I would go upstairs and see if Dad was safely asleep. The kitchen door was still open – it was a warm night – and Mum went out into the garden as I was going up the stairs.' He paused. 'Then I heard her scream and I ran straight down again. I went into the garden and she was kneeling by him. She said she thought he was dead and when I looked I could see that she was right.'

'How did you know he was dead, had you ever seen a dead body before?' Keith asked.

'No,' said Andrew, 'but his eyes were wide open, he was staring at nothing. His skin was cold to the touch, he wasn't breathing.'

'So, did you think about a doctor?'

Mother and son exchanged a look. 'Yes, of course we did,' said Andrew, 'we thought about calling a doctor, and we thought about calling the police.'

'So why didn't you?' Keith asked, his voice hardening.

'Because,' said Violet, 'because like I told you, dear, I thought Andy had killed him, I thought Andy would go to prison, I thought it would finish his young life. I couldn't bear that – he'd suffered enough already.'

'So what happened next?' Jack asked.

'I dug,' said Andrew, ' for hours it seemed, dug and dug and dug as deep as I could get it.'

'And what did you do, Violet?'

'I sat by David, I didn't know what else to do.'

'It was about two in the morning,' said Andrew, 'when I finished. We put him in the hole. It was ghastly, and then – well, we covered him up. He was buried so deep I never thought anyone would ever find the body.'

'The earth has a way of shifting,' said Keith, 'things often come up to the surface over time.' He leant back in his chair and studied them each in turn. 'And then you told everyone he had run off?'

'Yes,' said Violet, 'as I said to you the other day, dear, it was so easy. Nobody thought it was surprising, they all knew he wasn't a nice man and everyone just accepted it. Any day I expected a policeman to come to the door and say where had he gone, but nobody did.'

'And you say his boss accepted the situation without any problem?'

For the first time there was the hint of evasion. Keith picked it up immediately.

'Yes,' Violet said, eventually.

'There is something you're not telling me here, Violet,' Keith said. 'Do you want a break for a minute?'

She shook her head.

Jack took over. 'I imagine, Mr Symonds, that your mother will have told you that your father was shot, shot through the heart or very close to it, our pathologist thinks, judging by the way the ribs have been damaged.'

Andrew nodded.

'We have to ask you Mr Symonds, did you shoot your father?'

Andrew stood up, suddenly, violently. 'No I did not!' he said. 'I was only sixteen years old, but I tell you this, if someone had put a gun in my hand, I might well have done.'

'Andy!' Violet said, looking up at him with anguish.

The two policemen sat unmoved while Andrew paced backwards and forwards across the room. 'The things he did to my mother were terrible. I used to hear them when I was a little boy, hardly more than a baby – her crying, her whimpering, her pleading, occasionally her screaming – formed the fabric of my childhood – I hated him, I could have killed him, but I didn't.'

'Although he was a countryman,' Jack said, 'he didn't have a gun licence. Does that mean there wasn't a gun in the house?'

'No, there wasn't,' said Andrew, 'he'd been done for all sorts of drink-related offences – drink-driving, he'd smashed the windows in the pub, he'd assaulted people besides my mother, there was no way he would ever have got a gun licence even if he applied for one. He had the good sense at least to recognise there was no point in trying.'

'So did anybody close to you have a gun? A hunting rifle is what we're looking for.'

Mother and son exchanged a look.

'This architectural training, how was it funded then?' Keith asked, changing tack suddenly. It caught both of them by surprise.

'With David gone there was a lot of money saved on drink. I continued to scrimp and save and we managed it,' Violet began.

'I know the man was a drunk,' said Keith, 'but he couldn't have drunk the equivalent of seven years of architectural training. The fees would have been paid for back then, I recognise, but you still had to live – you trained in Manchester I understand?'

Andrew nodded. 'We're going to have to tell them Mother, there isn't any other way.'

'I think I'll go and make some coffee,' she said, quietly. Nobody stopped her as she stood up unsteadily and walked out of the room.

'Tell us what?' Keith asked.

'My father's boss was a farmer named Jago Emmery. He was a bachelor, his fiancée had run off with his best friend shortly before the wedding and it had left him bitter where women were concerned. He never married nor did he have any children. He put up with my father's nonsense for years, not because my father was a good worker – I imagine he was fairly dreadful and certainly unreliable – but because he felt sorry for my mother and, I suppose, for me. With my father gone, he was very good to my mother, he gave her work and helped her in lots of ways – when there was anything wrong with the cottage he used to send over workmen to repair it.'

'You're skirting around the edge of this story, Mr Symonds,' said Keith, 'I'm not getting the full picture.'

'They had an affair,' said Andrew, at last. 'It went on for the rest of their lives until Jago died. He put me through university and beyond. He did it because he loved Mother, but I think he was quite proud of me too. We got on well enough, I was so grateful to be around a gentle man, a gentleman in every way.'

'And did this affair between your mother and Jago begin before your father died?'

Andrew cleared his throat. 'I think it might have done, yes.'

'And did your father know?' Keith asked.

'I have absolutely no idea.'

'Could it have been the cause of his drunkenness and his abuse?'

Andrew shook his head vehemently. 'Absolutely not, Mother says the abuse started shortly after I was born, he didn't like anybody else in her life.'

'So he would have been very jealous if he had known about her relationship with this Jago Emmery?'

'Yes he would, but he didn't.' Andrew was becoming very agitated.

'Am I to assume that Jago Emmery had a hunting rifle?'

Andrew nodded.

'And you think he killed your father?'

Andrew nodded again.

'Did he tell you or your mother?'

'No, of course not,' said Andrew, getting up and starting to pace again. 'We didn't know that my father had been shot until you told us, Chief Inspector.'

'But that's not true, is it?' said Keith. 'There must have been a sizable hole in your father's chest and a considerable amount of blood.'

'Alright, alright,' said Andrew, 'we did realise he'd been shot.'

'And you knew who had shot him?'

'We guessed,' said Andrew.

At that moment Violet came into the room carrying four mugs of coffee on a tray. She all but dropped it. 'Andy, you're not telling them?'

'I have to Mother, I have to tell them

everything.'

Violet swayed; Keith quickly grabbed the tray, Jack dropped his notebook and gently lowered Violet into a chair.

'Honestly,' said Keith, crouching down so his eyes were level with Violet's. 'Honestly Violet, it's best we know the whole truth, we can't help you unless we know everything. You and Andy are so busy protecting each other, but it's not helping.'

'Jago was so good to us, he looked after us, he helped Andy get established, he did everything,' Violet said at last. 'If David had lived, Andy would be a farm worker like his father and I – well, one day David would have killed me, he was bound to have done.' Violet kept her eyes averted and as she spoke she clasped and reclasped her hands.

Keith let out a sigh. He stood up and began passing around the mugs of coffee.

'Why do you think Jago chose that night to kill your father?' Keith asked Andrew.

'I don't know, Mother doesn't know either. She had been quite badly beaten up the week before and had found it difficult to cover the bruises. There was a nasty one on her jawline, he probably would have seen that.'

'Did he see it, Violet?'

'Yes,' Violet managed to say, her voice barely audible.

'Did he ask you about it?'

'Yes,' she said again.

'Did you tell him?'

'No, I said I had fallen,' Violet whispered.

'Did he believe you?' Keith persisted.

'No,' she said. There was silence in the room, broken at last by Violet. 'He used to go out at night, Jago, he had nothing to stay home for in those days, he used to go shooting the odd pigeon or rabbit for the pot. It may have been just bad luck he had the rifle with him that day.'

'So did you honestly never discuss what happened?'

'No.' Both mother and son spoke at the same time.

'So you put your husband in the ground, you spread the story that he had run away to Australia and you never even asked Jago if it was him who had shot him?'

'No,' said Violet, suddenly some of her old sparkle returning. 'If I had asked him, if I had known what he had done, then I would have had to do something about it, wouldn't I? I'd have had to report it, wouldn't I? I'd have had to go and see you, you policemen and tell them what had happened. What I didn't know, I couldn't pass on, could I? It might not have been Jago, anyway.'

'It was Jago,' said Andrew, quietly, 'it had to

be, but it is true, the whole matter was never discussed.'

'But didn't he ask what had happened to the body?'

'No,' said Andrew.

'But he must have wondered. If the body had been discovered then he would have been implicated. He must have expected to be arrested at any time.'

'We never discussed it,' Violet said, 'I told him David had run away to Australia, he accepted it and that really is God's truth.'

Ten minutes later Keith and Jack were sitting glumly in the car. It had been arranged that Jack would go back and take formal statements. 'Those statements are going to take for ever,' he grumbled.

'If I were you I'd set aside a day for each of them. You'll have to take the statements separately, of course and we'll have to be on the look-out for inconsistencies.'

'You don't believe them then, sir?'

'Of course I believe them, and so do you, don't you?'

'Yes, I do,' said Jack, 'but what a mess.'

'What a mess,' Keith agreed.

'What will become of them, sir?'

'I'm going to go and see the "Super" – Andrew

was a minor at the time, Violet was an abused wife. They've convinced me at any rate that they had nothing to do with the murder of David Symonds, directly that is. The main suspect is dead and during his lifetime he never confessed to the crime. I can't see that there is much of a case to put together. It's just a question of whether Violet and Andrew should be prosecuted for withholding information and miscarriage of justice.'

'Can we get them off, sir, assuming that's what you think should happen?'

'I do think it's what should happen, but I think they may well be charged with something. It's not the trial in the court that concerns me so much for those two; I can't see them going to prison for what they did. It's trial by media that worries me, the publicity could kill Violet.' Keith sighed. 'Still, you get the statements, I'll talk to the "Super" and we'll see where we go from there.'

13

Keith sat at his desk consuming an utterly tasteless garage sandwich washed down by an equally revolting cup of brown liquid which was described by the station machine as coffee. There was a certain skill, he mused, in producing a sandwich which was so complete devoid of flavour. Having managed half, he put the other half in the bin and telephoned Horace Greenaway.

'I'm not handling the case and nobody has anything to tell you yet, anyway, Keith.'

'I know, I know,' said Keith, 'this is something else, well no, not something else, a related matter.'

'Go on,' said Horace, wearily.

'Christopher Drummond, was he a painter?'

'No, I told you he was a don at Cambridge.'

'Yes, I realise that,' said Keith, 'I'm not suggesting he was a painter and decorator, nor am I suggesting that he was a full-time artist. I'm simply asking whether he painted for pleasure or maybe occasional gain.'

'As a matter of fact,' said Horace, 'he did, not for gain I'm sure, he didn't need money but he painted watercolours and, in fact, I know he was tied up in some way with the cathedral – I think they sell his prints and cards for charity. Why?'

'Just wondered,' said Keith.

'Oh come on, old boy, you never "just wonder" anything. If I'm providing you with vital information, the least you can do is to tell me why – besides which, Christopher was not unknown to me.'

'The other victims of the painting thefts appear to have been painters themselves – not particularly well known, except for Adam Mayfield.'

'Now Adam Mayfield I do know,' said Horace, 'his work is excellent. So he was one of the victims?'

'Yes,' said Keith, 'it was Felicity Paradise who spotted the link.'

'Ah, the fair Felicity wins again. I don't know how on earth you would run your police station without her.'

'Sod off, Horace.'

'Done,' said Horace and the phone went dead.

Keith dialled Felicity's number. 'Are you in the mood for some humble pie?'

'That would be a first from you,' she said.

'Christopher Drummond was an amateur

artist, at least when I say amateur that is probably the wrong word. He painted pictures and sold them but just for charity; he didn't need the money. Watercolours, I believe. I understand his work is for sale in the shop in Truro cathedral.'

'So there is a link. I told you.'

'I know you told me and I know I didn't believe you, which is why I'm ringing up now to apologise and to give you this information. Have I suffered enough?'

'I suppose so,' said Felicity, reluctantly.

'So, I have a rather busy twenty-four hours coming up and I was wondering – it's most irregular, but you wouldn't like to find out if your victims have a common denominator – perhaps a teacher, a friend, someone who links you all together.'

'A mutual friend who is really an art thief?' He could hear the laughter in her voice.

'Precisely,' said Keith, undeterred. 'Exactly that sort of thing. This isn't my case so I can't really start muscling in on it, and what I should be doing is passing everything I know to DI Mavers who is running the investigation.'

'But since clearly you don't like him, you think it would be rather satisfying if we could be one step ahead of him?' Felicity suggested.

'What an appalling concept,' said Keith.

'And do I get any reward for all this

endeavour?'

'Lunch or supper of your choosing,' said Keith.

'Done deal,' Felicity replied.

It was rare for Keith Penrose and his sergeant to socialise but when Jack knocked on Keith's door he saw his boss sitting very forlornly and staring into space. Jack glanced at his watch; it was just after six.

'Sir, I've got some news on the taxi driver in relation to the Symonds case. I could tell you about it here or would you fancy a pint on the way home, given Mrs Penrose is away and all?'

From the look on Keith's face, Jack could tell he had made a good suggestion. 'What about Maggie though?' Keith asked.

'Her mother is staying with us for a few days, they'll be gassing half the night, they won't even notice I'm not there.'

'Great,' said Keith, 'let's go.' He stood up and picked up his jacket.

They went to Mannings at the bottom end of Lemon Street. Jack had a pint, Keith a small glass of red wine. 'So, what news on the taxi driver?' Keith asked.

'Jennings,' said Jack, 'he now lives in Northampton. He remembers the Symonds family well, said he felt sorry for young Andy who was a friend of his little brother, George. Of course, after all these years he can't tell us the date or even the year precisely but he does remember that evening, he does remember picking up mother and son outside Marazion and wondering what on earth they were doing trailing along so far from home. He also remembers there being a tension in the car and a reluctance to get out of it when he dropped them off at home. So, I guess where that leaves us sir, is that we can't prove that they ever went to Marazion, but they certainly came back from it.'

'If it was the right day, if it was even the right year… It is all very flimsy, Jack.'

'I think it's amazing he remembered it at all,' said Jack, 'it wasn't easy tracking him down and I was just so relieved that he even knew who the Symondses were.'

'Sorry,' said Keith, 'you're right, well done. It's just that somehow I've got to find a way to pitch this to the Super tomorrow. I know he already thinks I'm a soft git; he'll imagine Violet has wrapped me around her little finger and believe that the Symondses should be sent to the gallows for what they've done.'

'You can do it, sir,' said Jack, 'you can be quite eloquent when you try.'

'Blimey,' said Keith, 'is that a compliment?'

Jack smiled at him. 'Sort of.'

'The problem is,' said Keith, 'it so easily could be construed as a conspiracy.'

'What, the Symonds affair?'

Keith nodded. 'Violet was having an affair with Jago Emmery, her husband's boss. Her husband was, without doubt, a nasty piece of work – not only did he abuse her, but one suspects kept her and the boy in constant fear. Jago and Violet wanted to be together. Violet wanted Andy to have a decent future. With David out of the way, all these things were possible. So they conspired to murder him and bury him in the vegetable garden and no one would ever have known but for some over-zealous digging by the new owner many years later.'

'Do you think that's what happened?'

'No, I don't,' said Keith. 'I reckon it happened as they told it.'

'And my taxi driver does at least confirm they weren't around at the time of the shooting.'

'No, no, Jack, that's not true. You're assuming we're even talking about the same day. If Violet and Andy are involved in a cover-up, they could have remembered that Ian Jennings had picked them up one summer's evening – anytime from 1978 to 1980. They could have reckoned that all these years later he might remember the incident but not when it happened. It's circumstantial evidence; not even that, it's not evidence at all. You can't get away from the fact that when Violet realised her husband was dead, she also guessed who had murdered him. At that point she should have contacted the police; instead she saw Jago as her saviour too and went on to commit a serious crime.'

'It could have been planned but more likely, she saw it as the opportunity to start a new life,' Jack said.

'Exactly, but that doesn't make it right, does it? No one in any circumstances has the right to take another person's life. These abused women, I know it's terrible and I know in some circumstances they are too frightened to do anything about it, but in Violet's case, she is an articulate person. Why didn't she simply take her son and leave, why put up with the abuse all those years?'

'You're talking yourself out of this,' said Jack, 'you're not going to be helping them tomorrow by the look of it.'

'I am,' said Keith, 'I'm only playing devil's advocate, I'm only saying what I know the "Super" will say.' He stared glumly into the dregs of his wine. 'What I think happened,' he said at last, 'is when they first saw the body of David Symonds, mother and son assumed that he was dead because of Andy hitting him over the head. Therefore, they made the commitment to cover up his death to spare Andy. Then when they discovered he had been shot, they knew at once who had shot him, but they were too far down the line in their thinking to cover up the death and not contact the police, that they simply went ahead with it. They would have been in a blind panic, they weren't thinking straight and he was little more than a child. In my view, living with what they did has been punishment enough.' Keith glanced at his watch. 'It's nearly seven, time you were home, boy.'

'You're right, I'm probably pushing things a bit. It must be quite nice, sir, to have freedom, not feel you have to get back all the time.'

'Actually,' said Keith, 'it's damn lonely – remember that the next time Maggie tears you off a strip for being late for a meal, the alternative is much worse.'

Keith was half way through another microwaved shepherd's pie when the home phone rang. He was startled by it; he used the home phone so rarely that it had to be one of Barbara's friends. He got up and lifted the receiver. 'Keith Penrose.'

'Keith, it's Graham Crisp.' Keith's mind whirled.

'Graham…' he began, before remembering that this was the name of Carly's boyfriend. 'Oh Graham, how are you? Is everything alright?'

'Everyone is fine,' said Graham, 'how are you

doing left all alone?'

'I'm fine too, I'm just eating one of Barbara's shepherd's pies. Tell her it's delicious would you, from me?'

'I will of course and I'm sorry to disturb you in the middle of supper, only I'm an early riser and I wanted to have a word with you in private.'

Keith felt a rush of apprehension. 'Is everything alright, is Carly alright, she's not ill again?'

'No, no, nothing like that. I want to ask her to marry me, Keith, but I wanted to seek your permission first.'

There was a moment's stunned silence, then Keith rallied. 'That's extremely civil of you, Graham, thank you.'

'It is tradition,' Graham suggested. 'So?'

'So, what?' Keith asked, stupidly.

'Do I have your permission?'

'Of course you do,' said Keith. 'I'm sorry, I was just surprised, I don't know why – if I had thought about it, it is obvious it would be on the cards. Congratulations.'

'No congratulations yet,' said Graham, 'I haven't asked her, she might say no.'

'I very much doubt it,' said Keith.

'I don't think one can be at all sure,' said Graham, 'I'm incredibly nervous about it. She's a strong-minded woman, your daughter.'

'Takes after her mother,' said Keith. 'Well, good luck, boy, presumably somebody will let me know the outcome. I'll be thinking of you.'

'Thanks Keith, I'll try and be a decent son-in-law.'

'I'll try to be a decent father-in-law,' Keith promised. He replaced the receiver and returned to the kitchen table; somehow the shepherd's pie looked less appealing. He poured himself a glass of wine and sat at the table brooding. Of course he was pleased for Carly. Graham Crisp was a good chap with all the right instincts; he would look after Carly. It was no small thing to be taking her on: the threat of the return of her Hodgkins Lymphoma was always there and the possibility that she might be infertile after her treatment and then, of course, Graham was right, she was a very strong-minded young woman. Still, they had been together long enough now; Graham had to know what he was taking on. Suddenly the thought of where they were going to spend their married life came flooding into Keith's head. Now that they were marrying, would they stay out in Australia? It was something he should have asked but, then again, it had not been the right moment. How would he feel about Carly making her life in Australia, his grandchildren growing up there? One step at a time, he told himself firmly – Carly might turn him down yet.

14

Superintendent George Staple sat behind his desk having just finished re-reading the report Keith Penrose had sent him. It was typical of the man, of course. How he had managed to maintain such compassion over so many years in the police force never failed to surprise George. It was Keith Penrose's strength and it was also his weakness. He lifted the telephone. 'Send him in,' he said to his secretary.

The two men shook hands and George indicated a couple of easy chairs by the window. This was an encouraging sign – when a member of his team was in trouble, George Staple stayed behind his desk.

'So, Keith,' said George, fixing him with a steady and as always unnerving gaze. 'I'm prepared to back your hunch so far as the Symondses are concerned. I'll see what I can do to keep them out of court. No promises mind, but I'll have a try.'

'I do appreciate that, sir,' said Keith, mightily

relieved. He had been expecting a fight.

'It's not up to me to question your judgement in this instance. You've been around long enough to know when you're being taken for a ride. I just hope you haven't missed anything.'

'I don't think so, sir,' said Keith. 'I took along my sergeant for the full interview; he's far more world-weary than me and is of the same view that they are telling the truth.'

George smiled at him. 'That's your trouble isn't it Keith? You're not at all world-weary – you damn well should be, but you're not. You're still one of life's enthusiasts, God knows why.'

'I love my job,' said Keith, 'I love trying to sort things out. The older I get, like all of us I suppose, sir, I see everything far less in black and white and more in shades of grey.'

'So you're saying the line between villains and victims becomes ever more fuzzy?'

'Not exactly,' said Keith. 'Breaking the law is still breaking the law, but understanding why it has been broken, as in this case, that's the interesting bit.'

'What the hell are you going to do when you retire, Keith?' George asked.

Keith smiled at him. 'I've no idea, sir, I'm just blanking it out at the moment.'

'I bet your wife is dreading it, you'll be awful

to live with.'

'She has said much the same thing, sir, several times.'

'How is Barbara? I am amazed she still puts up with you after all these years.'

'She's coping – just. Actually, she's gone to Australia to see our daughter, who worryingly looks like she might be going to settle out there.'

'Don't blame her,' said George.

'That's the trouble,' said Keith, 'neither do I.' There was bleakness in his voice that did not escape his boss.

'All we can do is teach them to fly, Keith.'

Keith smiled at him. 'I know, sir, but it doesn't make it any easier though, does it?'

'So was there anything else you wanted to see me about?' George asked.

'Yes,' said Keith, 'about the Irvings.'

Immediately a mask fell over George's face. 'I thought we had agreed...'

'We have agreed, sir, and I'm not going to cause any trouble, it's just that I know what's happened.'

George Staple stood up abruptly and retreated behind his desk, not a good sign. 'And what is it you think you know?'

Keith stood up too and came to stand in front of George, like an erring schoolboy. 'I know that Sir

Hugo has defected to Russia.'

Sir Hugo is dead.'

'No, he isn't, I know he's not dead. The body in the family graveyard is that of Bob Barnes the uncle. Sir Hugo has been masquerading as Bob ever since his brother's murder. Then a few days ago, last week in fact, he defected. All I wondered was, how it was going to affect the family – do they need protection of any kind?'

'May I ask how you know all this?'

Keith shook his head. 'No sir.'

'And if I order you to tell me?'

'I would say, sir, that there are times when confidences just cannot be betrayed.'

George stared at Keith for some long moments, frowning. Suddenly his expression cleared. 'The boy, it's the boy, Miles, he told you. You have a soft spot for that young chap, don't you?'

'I'm worried about him and his mother, will they be safe?'

'I don't know any more than you,' George Staple said. 'As you know, we were warned off the case and I can confirm that I have received notification that the whole affair is now finally concluded, because of Sir Hugo's defection. Obviously, it is classified information, because everyone thinks Sir Hugo is dead. The boy shouldn't have told you.'

'So who killed Bob Barnes?' said Keith. 'Was it us or the Russians and why?'

'Keith, you're just stepping out of line again. There is nothing more to be said in the case of the Irvings. I will never discuss them again. Do you understand?'

'Did he grill you alive?' Jack asked, as he passed his boss in the corridor en route to his office.

'Surprisingly not,' said Keith. 'He's going to give the case his best shot to try and get the Symondes off the hook.'

'Blimey, what's happened to him – double lobotomy or something?'

'A little more respect towards your superintendent would not go amiss, Jack.'

'So the old boy was in good form,' said Jack, unrepentant.

Keith simply nodded. 'Anything for me?'

'No,' said Jack, 'I'm just off to Bedford Road, I've done Andrew's statement so he can go home, and I'm now going to tackle Violet.'

'Any problems with Andrew's?'

'Not at all,' said Jack, 'in fact he came across as a much nicer bloke than I had anticipated. Burying his father has blighted his whole life. As you said, he's more than suffered for that awful error of judgement.'

'And he was only sixteen,' said Keith.

'And he was only sixteen,' Jack agreed. 'I've had a call from Horace, too.'

'Doctor Greenaway to you,' said Keith. 'What did he want?'

'He was ringing to confirm that the relationship between Andrew Symonds and the skeleton was that of father and son, therefore the skeleton is indeed David Symonds.'

'Did you tell him we were way ahead of him?'

'I didn't sir,' said Jack, smiling. 'I rather thought I'd leave that pleasure to you.'

Jan Shankland's house in Carbis Bay was easy to find. Its position was magnificent, with views of the Hayle estuary to the right and St Ives to the left. There was a huge conservatory which dominated the back of the house to maximise the view and below the conservatory, a terrace and swimming pool. Having seated Felicity in the conservatory, Jan disappeared and returned with a coffee percolator. Felicity's excuse for calling was to commiserate with a fellow sufferer. Jan, she had learnt, had lost a Terry Frost painting.

'It was terrible,' she told Felicity, waving her arms theatrically. She looked so urban and totally out of place in Carbis Bay, with perfect hair and make-up and bright red fingernails. Felicity judged her to be in her fifties, but she was wearing leopard-skin leggings, a sort of silky black top and huge hooped earrings – it's only eleven o'clock in the morning for God's sake, Felicity thought. 'I'm sure it was,' she answered, sweetly.

'It's such a shock someone breaking into your home. Alan, my husband, still works up in London so he's only down at weekends,' Jan continued, 'so I was here on my own.'

'They broke in while you were here?' said Felicity, thinking of the fate of poor Christopher Drummond.

'No, I was out for dinner in St Ives with some girlfriends, thank God. The police rang me because my alarm was going off, not that the thieves cared, they simply broke down the door, took the painting and went. They were long gone before the police were anywhere near.'

'Same with me,' said Felicity.

'And you live in St Ives, you'd have thought your neighbours would have heard the alarm.'

Felicity shifted in her chair uneasily. 'I didn't have an alarm.'

'What, no alarm to your house?'

'No,' said Felicity. 'I very often forget to lock the front door.'

'Goodness, so was it a valuable painting taken?'

'A Constable,' said Felicity, 'only a little one.'

'And you didn't have it alarmed?'

Felicity bit her tongue. It was very tempting to remind this woman that an alarm had done her no good. Instinctively she didn't like her; they had nothing in common but she needed to ingratiate herself. She turned her attention to the house, complimenting her on this and that. There was a great deal of glass and chrome which appealed to Felicity not at all, but the view was magnificent and she homed in on that.

'I was wondering,' said Felicity at last, small talk exhausted, 'whether we have anything in common, a common link.'

'What do you mean?' Jan asked, looking startled; clearly less than enthusiastic about having anything in common with Felicity.

'Well, in both cases, yours and mine, the thief knew what he, or I suppose she, was looking for. Therefore he or she knew both the layout of our houses and the fact that we each owned a valuable painting.'

'So what are you saying?' Jan asked.

Felicity bit back her irritation. This woman was being unbelievably thick. 'Maybe there is someone we both know, someone who we've let into our house, or told them about our paintings and that person could be either the thief or the person who informed the thief. I'm looking for a common denominator, Jan.'

'That's the police's job surely, isn't it?' said Jan.

'The police haven't lost the paintings, we're the people who have suffered. I thought it was worth coming around to see you to say how sorry I am, but also to see whether we could try to find that thing we have in common. A friend, maybe?'

'None of my friends would steal my paintings,' said Jan, clearly affronted.

Felicity took a deep breath to control her mounting irritation. 'OK, let's look at this another way. How many people know you had a Terry Frost?'

'Hundreds,' said Jan, expansively. 'Alan is a very successful businessman. He is always bringing people down for the weekend, and we're making loads of friends locally. Anyone who has been to our house would have seen it, it was in our dining room. You can't miss it, couldn't miss it,' she corrected herself.

'Should we write a list of friends and acquaintances who have been to our respective houses and see if we find one in common? Felicity suggested.

'I'm not doing that,' said Jan. 'I know my friends, none of my friends would do such a thing, even if yours would.'

What a miserable cow, Felicity thought; though when she considered her iown mmediate friends, she had to admit it was ludicrous to suppose any of them were into art theft.

'We do have the St Ives School of Art in common,' Felicity said, trying to steer Jan away from the supposed insult to her friends.

'I've never told anybody there I have a Terry Frost.'

And I've never told anybody there I had a Constable, thought Felicity gloomily. 'Alright, not that, the school then, anything else we might have in common?'

'No, I'm sorry, I'm not liking this conversation. I don't want to be unkind but I think you should leave now. I don't like it being suggested my friends are thieves.'

'I was only trying to help,' Felicity protested, as she was ushered out of the door. It's people like that who give incomers a bad name, Felicity thought savagely as she marched away from the ghastly ornate porch towards her parked car.

Adam Mayfield will be a completely different kettle of fish, Felicity thought as she drove into Penzance. She had tried telephoning him several times over the last twenty-four hours, but without success. He simply didn't answer his phone or else, possibly, he was away. Trying to talk to him would be hampered by the fact that she greatly admired him, at least his work, and she was therefore deeply in awe of him. His great seascapes, his rugged moorlands, his granite cliffs completely encapsulated everything for which West Cornwall stood – at least in Felicity's eyes. He had the light just right, which so many artists failed to do. He painted it as he saw it and as he saw it, he clearly loved it. His love for his part of Cornwall just poured out of his paintings and as a result, she felt totally intimidated at the prospect of meeting him.

His home was a shabby old Victorian house that had known better days. It reminded her very much of the Victorian houses in North Oxford, the difference being that because it was Penzance, there was a large palm tree in the garden. She parked the car and walked up to a front door that could have done with a lick of paint some ten years previously. There didn't appear to be a bell so she rapped on the knocker. There was a very long silence and she wondered whether she should knock again or accept the fact that he wasn't in. She was still deliberating when she heard footsteps and the door opened. A strange but rather splendid creature was standing in the doorway. She was a small woman but as wide as she was tall, her grey hair was in dreadlocks secured with colourful wraps and she wore a long-sleeved, floor-length garment, which Felicity seemed to remember was called a kaftan. It was covered in brocade, shells and cut glass and on her feet were a pair of magnificent purple baseball boots which Felicity immediately envied.

'Mrs Mayfield?' she suggested.

'Good Lord, no,' was the reply. 'I wouldn't marry him, to marry him you would have to be completely off your rocker! What do you want anyway?' An interesting start.

'My name is Felicity Paradise,' she began.

'It can't be,' was the reply.

'Why?' Felicity asked.

'Well, no one is called that, are they, sensibly.'

'I promise you I am,' said Felicity, who was no stranger to ridicule concerning her name. 'And you are?'

'My name is Mabel, I'm his housekeeper, though God knows why I put up with him.'

'I'm here about the theft of his painting,' Felicity ploughed on.

'Are you the police then? You don't look like it.'

'No, I'm not,' said Felicity. 'I'm a fellow sufferer, I had a painting stolen from St Ives about a week before Mr Mayfield. I just wondered if I could talk to him about it, wondered if we could think of anything we have in common which might give us a clue as to the identity of the thief.'

'He doesn't like talking about it,' said Mabel.

'I'm sure he doesn't; neither do I but we want our paintings back, don't we? What did he have taken?'

'A Picasso,' said Mabel, 'and he goes into a rage every time you mention it. I don't fancy your chances but you can try and talk to him if you want. He hasn't painted since the theft, he sits in his studio and broods – an absolute pain in the ass, I can tell you.'

Adam Mayfield was indeed hunched in his armchair in his studio in front of a log-burning stove; his chair was draped with a tartan rug and a matching rug was placed over his knees. Felicity knew him to be in his early sixties but he looked much older. His hair was completely white, though still bushy and vigorous in growth, he had huge shaggy eyebrows and underneath these was a pair of blue eyes which regarded her with considerable scepticism.

'I'm sorry to intrude,' Felicity said.

'This here,' said Mabel, 'is Felicity Paradise, would you believe. She wants to talk to you about the theft.'

'I'm not talking to anybody about the theft,' said Adam Mayfield.

'Please,' said Felicity, 'I lost a painting too, a

Constable, about two weeks ago.'

At the mention of the Constable, he lifted his head and met her eye. Seizing the initiative, Felicity grabbed a chair and drew it close to him, sitting beside him in front of the fire.

'The police are useless,' she said, sensing this might be the right way in. 'I just thought maybe we could compare notes, work out what or who we have in common, someone we both know who might have been aware we owned valuable paintings.'

'I don't have friends anymore,' said Adam Mayfield, 'can't be doing with them. Anyway, *she* puts them off, she won't let anyone near me but her. She's my gaoler, I am a prisoner in my own home. I can't stand the woman.'

'I can't stand you either,' said Mabel.

Felicity suppressed a smile. It was obvious already that these two were devoted to one another, they just had a funny way of showing it. 'OK, so no friends,' she said briskly, 'but has anybody come to the house recently who might have seen your Picasso?'

'How do you know I had a Picasso stolen?' Adam demanded.

'Mabel told me,' said Felicity.

'Blabbermouth!' shouted Adam. 'Will you ever learn to keep your mouth shut, woman?'

'Don't you dare speak to me like that, you old fool!' said Mabel and stormed out of the room.

'I know it must be an awful loss to you,' said Felicity, after a pause to let the dust settle, 'and I'm sorry to drag it all up.'

'I knew him as a boy, you see,' said Adam.

'Who, Picasso?'

'Yes, my parents rented a house in the South of France and we just happened to be next door to where he was staying. I was only a kid but I was already spending every waking moment drawing and painting. He was so kind to me, helped me, encouraged me. My father had no time for my "scribbling" as he called it. Pablo, he understood. The painting, as you called it, was just a little sketch. He gave it to me when I left. It was years before I found anyone else who understood me as he did – come to think of it I don't think anybody ever has. I know it's worth a fortune now, but that's not the point.'

'I'm so sorry,' said Felicity.

'Yes, well,' said Adam, staring into the fire.

'My story is different but not unsimilar in some ways,' said Felicity. 'My husband's mother's family owned a big estate in Herefordshire. There was a mess-up with death duties and taxes and they lost everything, went bankrupt, everything had to be sold. However, my mother-in-law had been given this little Constable by her parents for her twenty-first birthday and she was allowed to keep it. She married a South African, who turned out to be no good.'

'South African men have a tendency that way,' said Adam darkly.

Felicity ignored him. 'They had just the one child, my husband, and then his father left them and returned to South Africa. They were very poor, mother and son, but they didn't sell the Constable, they kept it. My husband died in a hit-and-run in Oxford some years ago; well, seven years ago. I inherited the painting and was keeping it for my children. I was so stupid and I don't have an alarm for my cottage in St Ives, or for the painting, it just never occurred to me.'

For the first time Adam looked at her properly. 'No, I don't go in for any of that stuff either,' he said, 'in fact I don't think we've got a key for this house.'

Felicity smiled at him. 'I never remember to lock my door either.'

'It's sad,' said Adam, 'those days are coming to an end, even in Cornwall. We should know that after what's happened to us over the last few weeks. How about a glass of wine, would that be a good idea?'

'It would be a wonderful idea,' said Felicity.

'Mabel,' Adam shouted. Mabel, who had clearly been listening outside the door, appeared instantly. 'A bottle of wine and two glasses.'

'You can have a bottle of wine and three glasses,' said Mabel.

'I don't want you interfering, I'm having a good talk with this lovely young lady. You go and scrub something, prepare dinner, I don't know – do whatever it is you do.'

'You're a miserable old sod,' said Mabel, but not without affection. She returned, as ordered, with a chilled bottle of rosé and two glasses.

'Are you really not joining us?' Felicity asked.

'No,' said Mabel, 'it'll do him good to have a bit of company. Call me if he gets annoying.'

Adam poured wine into their glasses and they began to talk about artists. Felicity told him about her life in Oxford and he told her about his raucous youth. 'I've been everywhere,' he said, 'Paris, of course, Barcelona, Berlin, I've travelled in Spain, Greece and Italy and France but it wasn't until my forties I saw sense.'

'What happened in your forties?' Felicity said.

'I came here, and I rented a cottage from a friend in Nancledra. I arrived in the dark, there was no electricity or hot water, I was cold and hungry, I wrapped myself up in an old sleeping bag. It was May. The following morning I woke up at dawn. I'd been told there was a legendary pub at Zennor, I looked on a map and decided to walk there. I went up over the moor and as I came down the other side and saw the sea laid out before me and the cliffs, I knew I'd come home, I knew I'd never leave again and I never have.'

'So why are you in Penzance and not in Zennor, which I would have thought was more your sort of place?'

'This is Mabel's house,' Adam said, simply. 'I've had four wives, God knows how many children, several mistresses, several bastards and I haven't a penny to my name. Mabel showed unusual compassion and took me in when the bailiffs removed my last stick of furniture and my last painting.'

'But they didn't get the Picasso?'

'No, my God, they didn't,' said Adam, 'that was already here at Mabel's, no they bloody didn't get it, and now look what's happened.' More wine was poured and he began to flirt with her gently. 'If I was twenty years younger,' he said, 'you'd be just my sort.'

'Ten would do it actually,' said Felicity, smiling.

He laughed. 'You flatter me.'

'I expect,' said Felicity, 'that you don't need anybody in the world but Mabel.'

He sobered suddenly. 'You're right, she's my

rock, she's the only good woman I've ever loved, the rest…' He shrugged his shoulders.

'Then you're a lucky man.'

'I am,' he said, 'but don't for Christ's sake tell her.' The wine continued to flow and Felicity was increasingly conscious that she had to drive home.

'I need to stop drinking,' she said firmly, 'I'm supposed to be interrogating you as to what we have in common. We have a fellow sufferer, I saw her this morning. She lives in Carbis Bay and is rather terrifyingly well-groomed. Her name is Jan Shankland and she lost a Terry Frost.'

'A painting of Terry's – that's awful.'

'You knew him then?' Felicity asked.

'Yes, of course I did, knew him well and admired his work tremendously.'

'But you are so different as artists,' Felicity protested, 'you so traditional, him so abstract.'

'Aah, my dear Felicity, you are overlooking the most important thing we had in common,' Adam said.

'Which is?'

'Our love of Cornwall, naturally. He was extreme, had to stand on the edge of every cliff, swim as deep as he could… it killed him of course. A wonderful man, a wonderful artist. I hope this woman deserved to have one of his paintings.'

'I rather imagine you would think not,' said

Felicity with a smile. 'Listen, I must go.'

'You're having a nice time though, aren't you?' said Adam.

'I am, but I was very frightened about meeting you,' Felicity admitted.

'Really, why was that?'

'Well, I've admired your work for years, I'm a sort of groupie.'

'Now that is the way to worm your way into an old man's heart.'

Felicity laughed and stood up to go. 'It happens to be true. Where do you sell your work now?' she asked as she put on her coat.

'I don't paint much now,' said Adam. 'I send the odd painting up to London, I have an agent and a couple of friendly galleries up there.'

'And locally, do you sell anything locally?'

'No, the local galleries are no use these days, they're just interested in selling tat to tourists.'

She didn't know what made her say it. 'What about the Windward Gallery just down the road from you here?'

'That upstart, he came to see me, said he would fill his gallery with my paintings but only on sale or return. I told him to get stuffed. Give the old man a kiss.'

She kissed him on the cheek. 'Thanks for your time, it's been a real pleasure to meet you.'

'And you, my darling, take care.'

'He didn't eat me alive,' said Felicity as she threaded her way back to the kitchen where Mabel appeared to be tackling a mound of potatoes.

'You're his sort,' said Mabel, smiling. There was no rancour in her tone.

'He made me drink far too much wine. Would you mind if I left my car here for a little while and had a walk to clear my head?'

'Do you want some coffee?' Mabel asked.

'No, I'll be fine, a walk will sort me out.'

'I'll see you out then,' said Mabel.

'I envy you two,' said Felicity, on the spur of the moment as she reached the front door.

'Why's that then?' Mabel asked.

'Seeing you two together, I miss the camaraderie I suppose.'

'Camaraderie, what him and me?'

'Oh come off it, Mabel, you love him to bits and he loves you. Charlie, my husband, he and I, we used to be a little like you two, always having a go at each other but it was all good fun and there was lots of love underneath it all.'

'Was?' Mabel asked.

'He died,' said Felicity. 'It was just that some element of your relationship reminded me of us.'

'So what you're saying is I'm a lucky old trout and shouldn't forget it.'

Felicity smiled at her. 'Something like that.'

As soon as she was clear of the Mayfield house she dialled Jan Shankland's number.

'Jan, it's Felicity Paradise, we met this morning.'

'Yes,' said Jan, guardedly, 'I said I have nothing to tell you and I can't be long, my husband is back.'

'Just a quick one,' said Felicity. 'Have you ever sold any work? I know you do life classes, but do you actually sell your work?'

'I do a little,' said Jan.

'Where do you sell it?'

'To the Windward Gallery,' she said, 'in Penzance. Why?'

'I think they are our common denominator,' said Felicity.

15

'Dad!'

Keith was still struggling out of the depths of sleep. He squinted at his alarm clock, it was 5.45 in the morning. 'Carly, are you alright?'

'Of course I'm alright. Graham has asked me to marry him and I've said yes – of course I've said yes.'

Keith pulled himself up in the bed and tried to get his brain into gear. 'You said yes, brilliant, I am pleased for you, darling. You're happy about it?'

'Of course I'm happy about it Dad, I'm ecstatic. I gather you were in on it. Wasn't that lovely of Graham, asking you first? Very old-fashioned but very nice.'

'I agree,' said Keith, and he meant it. 'As long as you are happy, darling, that's all that matters to me. He's a very lucky chap.'

'Thanks Dad, I love you.'

'I love you too, Carly. So when's the wedding and more to the point where's the wedding?'

'Well, there is no point in hanging around, we don't want a big thing. We'd like to have it on the beach, we thought in February.'

Keith frowned, still trying to collect his thoughts. 'So,' he said, 'a beach in February, I take it we're looking at Australia rather than Cornwall.'

'You've got it, Dad,' said Carly with a laugh. 'You'll come out, won't you, you will come and give me away and all that?'

'Of course I will,' said Keith, 'your mother and I will both be there, and Will, I'll make sure Will comes too.'

'That's great Dad. Mum wants to speak to you. I'm so happy Dad, I can't believe it.'

'I'm glad, I'm so glad,' said Keith.

'Hello Keith,' said Barbara, 'it's wonderful news, isn't it?'

'Yes it is,' said Keith, 'you're happy about it?'

'I certainly am. Having seen something of this young man' (Graham was obviously in the room) 'I couldn't be more happy for Carly. You will come out for the wedding, won't you?'

'Of course I will,' said Keith, 'we can all travel together, you and me and Will.'

'That's what I wanted to talk to you about,' said Barbara. 'There doesn't seem much point in me coming home between now and the wedding.'

'How do you mean?' said Keith, stupidly.

'Well, I'd like to help Carly make all the arrangements for the wedding, that's what mothers do. I wasn't due to fly back home until early January, and Carly is talking about a wedding on Valentine's Day, the 14th of February, so it will save money and makes more sense for me to stay out until then. What do you think?'

Keith was astounded. 'Well, it's up to you,' he managed to get out the words, 'whatever you want. Can you afford to stay out there that long?'

'It's costing nothing, Keith, I'm staying with Carly and Graham and they're happy for me to do so. It makes absolutely no sense to pay for a flight to come home and then another one to come out again in a month's time. Also I really do want to help Carly with the wedding and I love it out here, absolutely love it.'

She sounded different, completely different. Keith felt slightly disorientated. 'You must do what you think is right, dear,' he said, 'it's fine with me, I'll be alright.'

'Are you sure? Carly is worried you'll starve, take to drink or go off the rails if I leave you alone.'

He laughed. 'I'll be fine, it's the obvious solution, it's a good idea…' He hesitated. 'Barbara, do you think they're going to stay out in Australia for good?'

'Of course they are, silly, what on earth have

they got to come home for?'

During the time she had been drinking wine with Adam Mayfield, it had grown dark. It was still only four o'clock, Felicity realised as she glanced at her watch, but it had been an overcast and blustery day. Having given Harvey a walk on the beach following her visit to Jan Shankland, she had decided to leave him at home, the cottage being a lot cosier than being stuck in the car all afternoon. She was extremely pleased with her decision now because by the time she reached the front, the wind coming off the sea was vicious and she had quite a job keeping upright. Harvey would have hated it.

There was no one to be seen as she forced her way along the windlashed pavement and then took the little lane off to the left which led up to the Windward Gallery. She was not quite sure what she was going to say when she got there, but at the moment all her concentration was channelled towards combating the appalling weather. The spray coming off the sea, combined with a sudden blustery shower, meant she was wet through by the time she reached the front of the gallery. The lights were all off, but then no one could blame them for closing on a night like this. She knew the only way into Tom and Sarah's flat was through the shop. Felicity took a step back and peered upwards, squinting, eyes streaming with water. The curtains were drawn. There appeared to be a light on but how to reach them and what to say if she did? – they'd think she was mad walking around Penzance in this weather. As she stood dithering by the door to the gallery, she suddenly realised there was a notice pinned to it. She stepped up close to the door which gave her a little shelter from the weather, wiped her eyes again and peered at the notice.

The Windward Gallery is now closed. The proprietors wish to thank all customers for their past support.

Closed. For a moment Felicity's brain, numbed by the cold, did not take in the implications of the sign but as she peered through the glass door it all became obvious. The shop had been completely cleared of stock. Anger bubbled up inside her. They had not paid for the last six paintings she had delivered, there were some cards too and half a dozen prints. She thought of the hours she had spent to produce the work. Damn them for trying to do a midnight flit! She moved out of the shelter of the doorway and again stared up at the flat above. Ring them, of course, that was the answer. She felt in her coat pocket and realised she had left her mobile phone in the car. She would go back to the car, telephone them and then drive round; she would either get the money off them or the paintings back. She couldn't believe it, she hadn't imagined they were that sort of people.

As she started down the alleyway which led back to the front, she was suddenly dazzled by headlights. A large car drove past her at speed, inches away, sending a wave of water all over her, completely drenching her from head to foot. It was the final straw. She turned and saw the car come to a halt in front of the gallery. A figure got out and began unlocking the front door. She turned around and began sloshing back towards the car.

'Hey,' she shouted, 'hey, wait a minute! Is that you, Tom?'

The lights went on in the gallery. The man standing in the doorway was certainly not Tom. He was a lot older; about Felicity's own age, she reckoned when she thought about it later; short, thick set and scowling at her.

'What do you want?' he said, belligerently.

'Well you can start by standing aside so I can get out of this rain,' said Felicity.

'You can't come in here,' he said.

'I certainly can.' said Felicity. 'I don't know who you are but the gallery owners have six of my paintings which they haven't paid for and I want them back.'

'Well, call them about it,' he said and before

Felicity knew what was happening, he gripped her by both shoulders, pushed her backwards and slammed the door in her face. She almost fell over but managed to steady herself. Rage, devoid of reason, swept over her. She began pummelling on the door.

'Open this door right now or I'm calling the police, and I'll keep shouting until you do,' she yelled. The door burst open again and the burly man on the other side grabbed her and pulled her in; she lost her footing, slipping and falling to the floor. It really hurt.

'Shut up you stupid bitch,' he shouted at her. He slammed the front door and locked it. Just at that moment there were footsteps on the stairs.

'What's going on?' Tom came running down the stairs. He looked at Felicity sprawled on the floor and went pale. 'Felicity, what on earth are you doing here?'

The thug replied for her. 'The stupid bitch started hammering and shouting at the door. Who the hell is she, anyway?'

Tom stared at Felicity who was trying to get to her feet, her knee and shoulder both hurting. 'She's no one, Greg,' Tom said. 'She's just one of our artists, there is nothing to worry about.'

'There is something to worry about,' said Felicity, now more or less on her feet, still bristling with anger. 'If you're closing down I want my paintings back, Tom, and who on earth is this, this person pushing and shoving me around?' Her voice was wobbly,she noticed, but still she felt no fear.

'Your paintings have all sold,' said Tom. 'I'll send you a cheque for what I owe you. I'm sorry we didn't give you any notice we were closing the gallery, only trade has not been so good. We'd hoped for better sales in the lead up to Christmas.'

'If sales are not so good, how come you've sold all my paintings?'

'That is none of your business,' the Greg person said. 'Now just get out of here, do as the man says, he'll send you a cheque.'

Felicity stood her ground and looked from one to the other. Tom looked pale and nervous, Greg looked as though he was about to do something violent; his fists were clenched and he had turned the colour of a tomato.

'Felicity, please,' Tom pleaded, 'just do as he says.'

'Not without knowing what is going on, Tom. Are you in some kind of trouble?'

'Yes,' said Tom, 'and you will be too if you don't do as Greg asks.'

'This is about the art thefts, isn't it? You bastard, you've got my Constable!' she burst out, 'and Adam Mayfield's Picasso and Jan Shankland's

Terry Frost and you...' her voice faltered, 'and you killed Christopher Drummond.' She looked from one to the other.

'That's enough!' said Greg. He grabbed Felicity by the arm and frogmarched her across the gallery. He pulled open the rear door and threw her in; this time she landed on concrete on her knees, scraping them badly. He slammed the door behind her and bolted it. She was in complete darkness.

Reeling from shock, she stayed where she was for a few moments. She could hear shouting on the other side of the door but could not make out what was being said. At last she got stiffly to her feet and groped her way to the wall. She began feeling her way along it and eventually came to a light switch which she turned on. She was in what was obviously the store room, but it too was completely empty, like the shop. It was not a good place to be locked away in – a concrete floor, bare walls, no chair or indeed anything at all – but it was at least dry. What was going to become of her? She took off her wet coat and shook it, put it on the ground inside out and sat down. She was cold, wet and clearly in danger. It was hard to imagine Tom and Sarah involved in art theft, but not so the brutal Greg who seemed to take pleasure in hurting people. She thought about Christopher Drummond. She couldn't imagine Tom being violent, but it was easy to imagine Greg causing him to fall to his death. If so, what was Greg capable of doing to her? She shuddered with cold and fear.

The shouting had stopped now. Suddenly there was a click and the lights went out. There was the slamming of a door and the sound of a car driving off, presumably Greg's, followed shortly by the start of another engine which seemed to be coming from the rear of the storeroom in which she was sitting. She listened to the sound of the two cars driving off into the night and then there was nothing but silence.

She wasn't dead or seriously injured. Presumably much of the shouting had been about what to do with her and clearly they had decided to leave her locked up so that they could make their get away. Now what? she thought, tears springing into her eyes. What would become of Harvey left alone in the cottage? He would be wondering what on earth had happened to her, he would be hungry soon. If only she had her mobile phone. How stupid of them, she thought, not to check that I didn't have one with me. Then she remembered trying to make a call from the gallery once and Sarah telling her there was no reception – they weren't worried whether she had a mobile phone or not, it wouldn't have made any difference. How long would it be before anyone discovered her?

She forced herself to stand up and began feeling her way around the walls again until she reached the door into the shop. She yanked down the handle and pushed in the vain hope that it might give way, but it was still firmly bolted from the outside. In the brief period that the room had been lit she knew there was no other way out, nor was there a window. There must be people living around here, she thought. This room probably backs onto a cottage. If I make enough racket, someone will hear me, won't they? She realised there was no point in trying now, she could still hear the wind howling – nobody would hear her cry above that, besides which every sane person would be behind closed curtains enjoying a meal or watching a bit of television. At the thought, she began to cry in earnest. What was wrong with her, why had she antagonised Greg, why couldn't she have seen the situation for what it was and just backed away? That was always her trouble, she always jumped into every situation with both feet without thinking things through. She had only herself to blame for the predicament in which she found herself. Why had she come to the gallery in the first place? – because she suspected that something odd had been going on. When Greg had thrown her out of the door, why hadn't she just gone, gone back to Adam Mayfield's and rung the police? It was what any sane person would have done.

She got down on her hands and knees and groped her way around until she found her coat. Using this as a pillow, a very sodden pillow, she lay down on the hard concrete floor. It was freezing cold. She lay shivering, cursing her own stupidity until at last, through sheer exhaustion, she fell asleep.

15

It was Saturday morning. Keith had a day off, indeed the whole weekend off, and he just did not know what to do with himself. He ate his solitary breakfast, washed up and peered out of the window. A stormy night seemed to be turning itself into a and it was still raining; the wind, gale-force the night before, did not seem to have abated much – tidying up the garden was out of the question. He sat glumly at the kitchen table trying to think of a single thing he wanted to do. Barbara's being away had been quite an eye-opener and done him no harm, he recognised. He had always had one his fair share of chores around the house. He liked cooking, he enjoyed gardening, he knew how to put on a load of washing and change a baby's nappy, but he had never been involved with the organisation of the family, he realised now. He simply went along with the plan, did as he was told. Most of their friends were really Barbara's friends. He was not anti-social, he liked people but he was in the people business. By the time he got home at night all he really wanted to do was crash out in front of the television, dinner parties and the like were not his style. Without Barbara on hand to tell him what to do, he was at a loss. He felt no resentment about this – it was more the recognition that the fallout from his demanding job meant he had always left it to someone else to organise his free time.

He thought about going Christmas shopping but there was little point. He had agreed with the family that he would bring out Christmas presents when he travelled to Australia, and that they would have a mini-Christmas before the wedding for his benefit. So there was no rush – why not wait until the January sales, he thought, ever practical. Barbara had written all the Christmas cards and left them for him to post, which he would do. He would buy a bottle of whisky for Jack and a toy for the baby. Other than that the only person he was tempted to buy a present for was, of course, Felicity Paradise – but what, he had no idea. Maybe he should call her and find out how she was getting on in her discussions with the other people who had had a painting stolen, maybe they could meet up. He brightened visibly and dialled her mobile number. It went straight to voicemail. He then dialled her home number and was greeted by the answerphone. Maybe she was away for the weekend, maybe she had gone up to Oxford, maybe she was with her grandchildren or maybe she had just gone out shopping and left her mobile behind. He would go to St Ives and see if he could meet up with her; if not he would go and see the latest exhibition at the Tate and have a bit of lunch in the restaurant. That would use up most of the day.

He left his car on the Wharf, in a loading bay, and walked up to Felicity's cottage. He saw that the French windows leading out onto her balcony were shut, which was not a good sign; even in winter she liked them open. He knocked on the door. Immediately there was an explosion of noise as he heard Harvey roaring down the stairs, barking and whining, scratching at the door – it was most unlike Harvey; he never normally made such a fuss when anyone came to the door, he was so used to the coming and goings of Felicity's friends and family. He knocked again. Still nothing but the frenzied barking and scratching continued. Keith had a great deal of faith in the good common sense and natural instinct of animals and Harvey's reaction didn't seem right. The thought of breaking down the purple door once again was out of the question and in any event ludicrously over-dramatic. Felicity hadn't answered the phone, had left the dog behind while she went somewhere and the dog didn't like it – hardly a crisis. Then suddenly he remembered her spare key. He reached up to the hanging basket which hung to the left-hand side of her front door. He felt around the back and sure enough there was a key. With a sigh of relief he opened the door and Harvey shot out, saw who it was and began jumping up and down hysterically. Keith walked into the hall which smelt strongly of dog excrement. He switched on the hall light and frowned at the mess; again this was most unlike Harvey, who was the cleanest dog he had ever met. What was going on? Ignoring Harvey's frenzy he ran upstairs two at a time.

'Felicity,' he called. There was no one in the kitchen or the sitting room. He retraced his steps downstairs and checked both bedrooms which were empty. Then he looked at Harvey.

'You've been left alone a long time, boy, haven't you?' He went upstairs and found some newspaper and cleared up the mess. Harvey's food bowl was licked clean, as was the water bowl. He filled the water bowl and Harvey lapped with enthusiasm while Keith hunted round in the cupboards until he found some dog food. He poured some into Harvey's bowl and watched with increasing concern as Harvey wolfed the lot. The meal finished, dog and man studied each other for a moment.

'You've been alone overnight I would say,' Keith said. 'She would never do that to you, never.' He looked wildly around the room. There was a pad near the telephone and on it was written the name of Jan Shankland and a telephone number. Keith picked up the phone and dialled the number.

'Hello,' said Keith, 'is that Mrs Shankland?'

'Yes,' was the tentative reply.

'This is Chief Inspector Keith Penrose of Devon and Cornwall Constabulary. I'm trying to track down the whereabouts of Felicity Paradise. Please don't think she has done anything wrong, quite the contrary, we're just concerned for her safety. Has she been to see you?'

'Why yes,' said Jan, 'she came yesterday morning, we had a cup of coffee. She was hoping I could help her with these art thefts, but I'm afraid I couldn't.'

'Do you know where she was going next?'

'Yes,' Jan replied, 'she was going to see Adam Mayfield in Penzance, he'd had a painting taken too.'

'Thanks,' said Keith, 'thanks a lot. What time did she leave you?'

'About twelve I would think,' said Jan. 'Is she alright?'

'I'm sure she is,' said Keith, 'I just need to get hold of her in a hurry. Thanks for your help, bye.'

He found the telephone book and Adam Mayfield's number; he rang but there was no response. Armed with the address, he began hurrying down the stairs towards the door when there was a whine behind him.

'Oh Harvey,' he said, 'I suppose I can't leave you, can I? It's not fair, you're worried too. Come on, let's find your lead.'

Harvey pulled strongly as they left the house. Keith slithered down the steps of Mount Zion and headed to his car. Harvey had other ideas and headed for the beach.

'OK, two minutes,' said Keith. He stood impatiently watching Harvey run around the beach then called him, clipped on his lead again and put him in the back of the car. 'Oh Lord,' said Keith, 'you're a real sandy mess and I haven't even got a rug.' He climbed into the driver's seat and set out for Penzance.

The moment Keith turned into the driveway of the Mayfield house he was flooded with a sense of relief for there, parked, was Felicity's car. The feeling of relief was followed by one of irritation. He'd had to clear up all the dog mess, the back of his car was now covered in sand and he had spent a frantic hour worrying himself sick that something awful had happened to her. Still she was safe and that was all that mattered.

'Stay where you are, Harvey,' he said. At the front door he searched for a bell without success. Finally, he banged on the knocker.

The door was opened by a quite extraordinay-looking woman. 'Who are you?' she asked.

He ignored the question, not wanting to reveal his identity; he was feeling a fool enough as it was.

'I'm sorry to trouble you,' he said, 'I'm just trying to track down Felicity Paradise, I have her dog in the car.'

'She's not here,' said Mabel.

'She must be, that's her car,' said Keith.

'She left it here last night and never came back. We're worried about her. In fact, I've been talking to Adam, I think we should call the police. It was a rough night, I can't think where she got to. Are you a friend of hers?'

'No need to call the police,' said Keith and produced his warrant card. The mad-looking woman squinted at it. 'Keith Penrose, Chief Inspector,' Keith said helpfully. 'Can I have a word with Adam Mayfield – is he your husband?'

'No, certainly not,' said Mabel, without further comment.

He was shown into a studio where a man who he knew from photographs to be Adam Mayfield was standing in front of a canvas.

'Mabel, for Christ's sake, you know I don't have anyone in here when I'm working.'

'It's a policeman,' said Mabel, 'he's here about Felicity.'

'I told you not to call them yet, I told you she'd turn up.'

'I didn't call them,' said Mabel. 'Just stop shouting and listen for a minute.'

Keith crossed the room. 'I'm really sorry to disturb you at work, sir, but I'm worried about Felicity Paradise. I gather she was here yesterday and that her car is still parked in your driveway following her visit to you.'

'That's right,' said Adam, smiling. 'We had a lovely time, she is such a nice woman.'

'If you're saying that to make me jealous, it's not working,' said Mabel and thundered out of the room.

'Don't take any notice of her,' said Adam, 'I never do.'

'Felicity Paradise,' said Keith, trying to keep him on track, 'she left here…'

'About four,' Adam said, 'we had some wine together and she said that before she went home she would have a breath of fresh air.'

'And that was it, you didn't see her again?'

'No,' said Adam, 'she didn't come back for her car. We just imagined she had met a friend and decided to prolong her visit, maybe stay overnight.'

'You didn't think to call anybody?' Keith asked.

'She's a grown woman. Maybe having had a couple of glasses of wine, she met a friend, had a few more and she decided to stay the night. She would have assumed we wouldn't mind her car staying where it was, and she would have been right.'

'She left her dog alone all night,' said Keith, knowing he sounded ridiculous.

'How was I supposed to know that?' Adam asked, not unreasonably.

'Sorry, sorry,' said Keith, 'but there is something not right here. What did she say to you before she left, did she give you any clue as to where she was going?'

Adam thought. 'I don't think so,' he said.

'Would your wife…'

'She's not my wife, her name is Mabel.'

'Would Mabel have any idea?'

'I don't know, you could ask her, if you wish. Silly old bat may know something I don't.'

'Felicity could be in serious danger,' said Keith, his sense of panic rising.

Adam stared at him shrewdly. 'This isn't just a police matter, is it, you care about this woman? I don't blame you, you're a lucky chap. If I was younger…'

Keith held up his hand to silence him, his frustration unbearable. 'Please stop, are you absolutely, absolutely certain that you don't know where she went?'

Adam's expression sobered. At last, thought Keith, he is taking me seriously.

'She mentioned the Windward Gallery. The silly ass who runs it came here once and tried to persuade me to sell some of my paintings in his gallery. He had to be joking – it's full of tourist crap. I told him to get knotted.'

Keith's mind did a few somersaults. 'And you told her that just before she left here?' Adam nodded. 'Where is the Windward Gallery?'

'Bottom end of Chapel Street, just before you get to the front, off to the left. You can't miss it, old-fashioned sort of frontage – awfully twee, ghastly place.'

'Thanks,' said Keith, 'I'm sorry for all the hassle, it's just…'

'You don't have to explain,' Adam said, 'you get going.'

Keith almost crashed into Mabel on his exit from the front door. 'Where are you off to?' she asked.

'He'll explain,' Keith said. He jumped into the car. 'We'll find her, Harvey,' he said, more to comfort himself than the dog and roared off down the hill towards the front. He found the gallery straight away and parked right by the door. Even before he got out of the car he could see it was empty.

'Come on, Harvey, you'd better come with me,' he said. Man and dog surveyed the front of the shop, Keith reading the notice saying the gallery had closed down. So what's happened here, Keith thought. Are these people responsible for the art thefts and did Felicity stumble upon them, did they deal with her as they dealt with Christopher Drummond, is her body even now dumped somewhere? He felt himself go hot and then cold. 'Come on Harvey,' he said again. He walked down the left hand side of the building; there was nothing but a high stone wall and no way of getting into the back of the building. He retraced his steps and walked down the right hand side of the building, where there was a side window which looked into the gallery area and then another blank wall. This time the walk ended in a car-parking space which clearly belonged to the shop, but it was empty too.

They had started to retrace their steps then Harvey began to whimper and whine, sniffing along the edge of the building. 'What is it?' Keith said. Harvey took no notice; his tail began to wag, he whined and sniffed and then barked. Keith pulled him back round to the front of the building and surveyed it. The door was a very stout wooden affair with a small glass panel, too small – on his own there was no way he could break it down. The windows of the shop were made of bottle glass. The small panes would not give him entry and would cost a fortune to replace. He could call for back-up, but was he making a fool of himself? Felicity was probably back at home wondering who had kidnapped her dog. And yet he knew she wasn't and it was clear that Harvey did too.

He walked back to the side window – it was the only way in. He studied it for a moment and then returned to his car. He put a very reluctant Harvey, who began yelping, back in the car. He selected a large spanner from his toolbox and returning to the window, smashed it – glass went everywhere but luckily missed him. Gingerly he put his hand through and undid the window latch, then pulled himself up onto the window frame and jumped down into the gallery, ripping his trousers and gashing his knee as he did so. 'I'm too old for this,' he thought. There was clearly no one in the gallery. He went back to the front door, unlocked it and let Harvey out of the car. Harvey shot like a bullet through the front door of the shop and went straight to the door at the rear. He began whining, barking, wagging his tail and scratching at the door. Keith shifted the bolt with difficulty and slid open the door. As light shone into the storeroom he saw a body huddled against the wall. For a moment he couldn't move, he wanted to speak but no sound came, he was apparently paralysed with shock. Harvey shot through his legs and dashed up to the body and began jumping excitedly all over it.

The body moved. 'Harvey, Harvey, is that really you?' said Felicity Paradise.

17

Five minutes later they were in the midst of a full-scale row, emotions running high, caused no doubt by both the shock and the relief.

'I am not going to the hospital,' Felicity said, 'it's a waste of everyone's time.'

'The hospital is less than five minutes away,' said Keith, 'and just look at the state of you.' He had draped his jacket around her and turned the heating up to full in the car but she was deathly white, grey almost, and her teeth were chattering.

'There is nothing wrong with me that getting off these damp clothes and having a hot bath won't put right. Please, Keith, I don't want to go to hospital and be prodded about. I just want to go home, I feel horrible but I'll be fine once I get home.'

'I think you should be checked out, you probably have hypothermia.'

'I don't need checking,' said Felicity, and began to cry. 'Please, please, Keith.'

Keith slowed the car and put his hand on her shoulder. 'Don't cry, I don't want to upset you, I can't bear it if I've made you cry.'

'Then for God's sake, take me home.'

'I just need to stop these people before they get away with the paintings and I can't do that and look after you at the same time.'

'Then stop the car,' said Felicity, 'and make the calls you need to make. I'm fine, please.'

They were almost outside the hospital entrance but he did as he was asked and parked the car. 'Right, what are we looking for?' he asked.

Felicity shook her head. 'I don't know what you mean, Keith.'

'What sort of vehicle?'

'I don't know, I didn't see them drive off.'

'What did you see then?'

'Absolutely nothing but please don't be angry with me,' said Felicity, 'I'm doing my best.'

'Sorry, sorry,' he said, 'I'm not thinking straight; you see, I thought you were dead. Help me, darling, please.' The endearment slipped out before he could stop himself. He cleared his throat. 'Help me, tell me anything you can remember.'

'Well there are three of them. Tom Ward is the owner of the gallery and then there is Sarah, who I don't think is his wife, but is certainly his girlfriend and then there was this horrible bloke called Greg, short and thick-set, looks like a boxer. He kept throwing me about, and it hurt and I got the feeling he was positively enjoying himself.'

'Throwing you about?' Keith looked horrified.

'But not hurting me enough to need to go to hospital,' Felicity said, hurriedly. 'The Greg person arrived in a car, a big one, big, shiny and expensive.'

'What, like a Mercedes?' Keith asked.

'I don't know,' said Felicity, helplessly, 'it was silver.'

'So the paintings must have been taken either in that or more than likely in a van. Do Sarah and Tom have a van?'

'I don't know,' said Felicity, 'I got dragged into the shop and then thrown into the store. I'm sorry, Keith.' She began to cry again.

'No, it's me who should be sorry,' he said, 'I'm not handling this well.' He took her hand, but this did not seem to be enough. He put his arms round her and let her sob against his shoulder. At last the crying stopped. 'Give me five minutes and I'll make some calls.' He got out of the car, punching in some numbers on his mobile as he went.

She watched him as he marched up and down the pavement, gesticulating wildly. Harvey crawled through from the back of the car and onto her lap; she hugged his warm little body close to her. Keith had left the engine running with the heater blasting out warm air but the cold had gone right through to her bones – she couldn't imagine ever being warm again.

At last he returned to the car, climbed in and turned to face her. 'Are you alright?'

She nodded. 'Can we go home now?'

He smiled at her. 'Of course we can.'

'What's happened?' she asked through chattering teeth, her voice sounding strained and hoarse to her own ears.

'We're in luck, I think. I assumed they would be trying to get the paintings out of the country and therefore would go straight to Plymouth to catch the car ferry there, being the nearest exit point.'

'Yes, I suppose so,' said Felicity, tiredly, trying to concentrate.

'But, luckily with this awful weather, the ferries have been cancelled, so we are assuming they are probably heading for Southampton. The bad weather is coming in from the west and so the sailings from Southampton are still operating at the moment.'

'But you don't even know what to look for because I couldn't tell you anything,' Felicity wailed.

'Don't worry, we're on to it. I've dug Jack out from the bosom of his family and as soon as I have you properly settled, I'll go straight back to the

Station. We'll get them. What time do you think it was that they left last night?'

Felicity thought. 'About five, five thirty, so they could have gone to Plymouth first then travelled overnight and caught an early sailing from Southampton this morning.'

'Maybe,' said Keith, 'but they would spend some time wondering whether to wait at Plymouth until the weather improved or whether to go to Southampton. Driving would have been atrocious last night – I'm cautiously optimistic.'

He drove along the Wharf which was as close as he could get by car to Felicity's cottage. 'Can you walk?' he asked.

'Of course I can walk.' She stumbled as he helped her out of the car, her legs feeling so weak they hardly seemed to belong to her. 'Oh, look what a mess Harvey has made of your car,' she said. 'So you took him on the beach?'

'Harvey is the hero of this story,' said Keith, 'but I will tell you everything later. For now just concentrate on walking.' He put an arm around her to support her and they climbed the steps to Jericho Cottage.

By the time Felicity had soaked in a scalding bath and drunk about two pints of water, Keith had turned her kitchen into an operations room.

'Feeling better?' he said, standing up as she climbed the stairs to her kitchen. She still looked very pale. 'Can I fix you some tea and maybe toast?' he suggested.

She nodded and sat down in the chair; she still felt so stupidly weak.

'His real name, as we supposed, really is Tom Ward and the girl is Sarah Bertram,' Keith said, as he busied himself with the kettle. 'We have found out that neither of them have any form, but we've had their passport photos e-mailed over to Southampton and indeed to all the ports and airports. The villain we reckon is a chap called Greg Hardcastle. He...' Keith paused; Felicity was sitting staring at him, but barely concentrating. 'What is it?' he asked, 'what's wrong?'

'I'm sorry, I *am* interested in what you are saying, it's just...' She started to cry again.

He came and knelt beside her and put his arms around her. 'Tell me,' he whispered.

'I thought I was going to die in there, Keith. I thought I would never be in this room again, never see you or my family ever again. I couldn't imagine how anyone would ever make the connection, would realise where I was. I knew however loud I shouted no one would hear me. I tried this morning but my voice just bounced back at me off the walls. It's an old building, with very thick granite walls...

and my voice was getting so hoarse, I knew no one would hear me – ever.' Her voice trailed away. He hugged her tighter and she leant her head against his. 'You saved my life.'

'It was Harvey,' Keith murmured against her. 'Firstly, when I arrived here this morning there was Harvey pee and poo all over the hall and I knew that wasn't right, not for Harvey. Then he was clearly starving so I realised he hadn't been fed and there was no water in his bowl and I knew that meant you must have been away overnight – I couldn't see any circumstances in which you would leave him, unless something had gone wrong. I've been in a state of total panic ever since. I'm sorry, you must think my priorities have gone to hell fussing about these paintings, but it's not really about them – I just can't bear the thought of these people getting away with it, not after what they did to you and poor Christopher Drummond.'

Felicity nodded. 'You're quite right, of course. Amazing things, hugs, I feel better already. Let's have some toast.'

Keith left half an hour later, having tucked up Felicity in bed with Harvey and a hot water bottle. She was asleep in seconds. She assured him she wanted nobody and needed no one, but having shut the front door and put the spare key back in the hanging basket, he drove straight to Hayle.

He did not have Mel and Martin's telephone number with him, but he knew where they lived. Martin answered the door. 'Chief Inspector, how good to see you! Are you alright? You look a bit…'

'Bedraggled?' Keith suggested.

'Yes, something like that. Is everything alright, is Fizzy alright?'

'Yes, she's fine but could I come in and talk to you and your wife a moment?'

'Yes, of course, come along in.'

It was a scene of perfect domestic bliss and for a moment it took him back to a time when his own children were small. Minty was drawing at the kitchen table, her mother Mel was beside her spooning food into a robust-looking baby whom he knew to be Charlie.

'Hello,' she said, 'this is an unexpected pleasure.' Then a look of concern crossed her face. 'Is Mum alright?'

Keith nodded. 'Yes, yes she's fine.'

'But…' Mel said, clearly missing nothing.

Suddenly all the fear and exhaustion of the day crept up on him. 'Could I sit down for a moment?' he asked.

'Of course. What on earth have you done to your knee, do you realise you're bleeding?' Mel's look of scrutiny was very reminiscent of her mother.

'It's fine,' said Keith, 'I'm fine, but I would like

you to go over and keep an eye on your mother. She says she doesn't need anybody but you know what she's like.' He poured the story out to them, while they plied him with cups of tea and a piece of cake. Twice he had to leave them so that he could take calls from the Station. As soon as the baby was fed, Mel left the children to go to her mother. 'She is going to be really angry with me,' Keith said, as Mel was leaving, 'for telling you, I mean.'

'I think I can handle it,' Mel said. 'She should be very grateful to you, not angry, and I'll make sure I tell her that.'

Keith returned to the kitchen table and found himself with Minty on his knee and another hot cup of tea. Martin sat down beside him.

'You look absolutely knackered, Keith. You haven't got to go back to the Station now, have you?'

Keith nodded. 'I'm determined to catch those villains. Felicity could so easily have died in there, you know.'

Martin nodded. 'But surely everything that can be done is being done.'

'I just need to be certain,' said Keith, 'but thank you for this, it's been a port in an otherwise rather stormy day. Felicity was so upset and when I opened the door of the store and saw her lying there, I thought, I thought...' For a moment he feared he was going to break down but with enormous effort he managed to pull himself together. 'I thought she was dead,' he said.

Martin laid a hand on his arm. 'But she's not.'

'No.'

At the same moment that Keith was sitting in the kitchen with Martin, Greg Hardcastle drove a red VW van into the queue for loading on to the two o'clock ferry from Southampton. He had two passengers. After a brief but violent skirmish, all three were in custody and the van was impounded. It was just after four o'clock when Keith rang Felicity's landline from the Station with the news.

Mel answered. 'Oh, Keith, she's asleep again.'

'When she wakes up, can you tell her we've got them,' said Keith, 'both the villains and the paintings. I'm not sure yet about the Constable but the van is stashed to the gunwales with paintings of various sorts and there has to be a sporting chance of the Constable being one of them.'

'Who cares about the Constable?' said Mel. 'You and Mum are alright, that's all that matters.'

'Is she still angry with me?'

'When she woke briefly about an hour ago, she asked for you. She didn't sound even slightly angry.'

'Good. Her car and mobile phone are still in Penzance.'

'I know,' said Mel, 'I've rung Adam Mayfield and they are happy for the car to stay there as long as we want. I'll drop her over there when she is well enough to drive.'

'Send her...' Keith hesitated, 'send her my very good wishes.'

'I will and thanks again for what you did today.'

18

Keith was in his sitting room in front of a roaring fire, the Sunday papers spread all round him. All day he had wanted to ring her but felt he would be intruding. Undoubtedly, being a Sunday, Mel would have taken her over to Hayle for Sunday lunch; being with the children would do her good. He glanced at his watch; it was 6.50. He imagined Mel would be bathing the children while Martin brought Felicity home.

He rang her number and she picked up almost immediately. 'I thought it might be you,' she said. 'Have you tried before? I've been out all day.'

'At Hayle?' he said.

'Yes, I spent the day with the children, it was lovely. It was extremely bad of you to involve Mel yesterday. You promised you wouldn't.'

'I couldn't leave you on your own,' Keith said, 'it was as simple as that. I just had to do it. Now, on a more positive note, you may remember that we had an agreement. If you solved the whereabouts of the missing paintings – and I think we can justifiably say that you have – I solemnly promised to take you out for a lunch or dinner of your choice.'

'I'm not sure,' said Felicity.

His heart sank. Where had he gone wrong? Their relationship was so complex, it was like walking through a minefield.

'It's not that I don't want to see you,' she said, 'it's just that I don't feel much like going out at the moment – maybe in a few days.'

'It's Christmas in a few days,' said Keith, 'I'm travelling up to Reading on the twenty-third and I'm spending Christmas with my sister. I was thinking about Tuesday evening, the twenty-second, I should be able to get away early provided there is no mischief abroad. Why don't I take you out to the Porthminster? You deserve a treat.'

'You couldn't come here, could you?' said Felicity. 'Come and have dinner with me.'

'That's hardly a treat.'

'You can bring a bottle,' said Felicity, 'I just don't feel like venturing out much at the moment, I hope you understand.'

'Are you sure you want me to come? We can leave it until after Christmas if you prefer.'

'No, no, it would be very good to see you.'

For some reason Keith felt ridiculously nervous, as

if he was eighteen and it was a first date. He didn't know what to do about the wine – she liked white and he liked red – so he had bought a bottle of each, far too expensive but hopefully good. He didn't know what to wear either, he spent so much of his life in a suit. In the end he found a half-decent checked shirt and a pair of jeans, then he thought he was underdressed for going out to dinner and changed the jeans for a pair of cords. He arrived in St Ives much too early and went to The Sloop and had half a pint to kill the time.

She answered the door in one of her mad sweaters and a pair of leggings, kissed him on the cheek and led him upstairs. 'Open the wine would you, Keith? I'll just check the oven, we've just a casserole and some cheese, is that alright?'

'Perfect,' he said looking around the cosy kitchen, 'you're quite right, this is much nicer than going out.'

'I thought so.'

He poured a glass of red and a glass of white and handed the white to her. 'I have a toast for you,' he said.

'Yes?' she said expectantly.

'To the safe return of the Constable.'

Felicity let out a scream, put down her wine glass and threw her arms around Keith's neck, nearly knocking the glass out of his own hand.

'Truly, is it found?' She drew away and studied his face. 'Honestly?'

'Honestly,' he said. 'It will take a week or two before it comes home, but it is safe.'

'And what about the Picasso?'

'That too, though they had some difficulty identifying that one. It's not at all his normal sort of thing – you know, the nose where the eye should be. This one is rather a lovely and very simple sketch of a dove.'

'It was drawn for a little boy,' said Felicity.

'Who, Adam?'

'Yes, Picasso drew it for him when Adam was a rather lonely and misunderstood child.'

'Then that would have been a very special picture to lose.'

Felicity nodded. 'And that Shankland woman's Terry Frost?'

'That too,' Keith assured her, 'all safe and well.'

The casserole was consumed, wine flowed; there was much to catch up on.

'Carly is getting married on the fourteenth of February,' Keith announced.

'Really? Congratulations, are you happy about it?'

He frowned. 'Yes, yes, I am happy – he is a nice chap, Graham, from what I know of him, a bit dull maybe but then Carly, like your Mel, is a fairly strong-minded young woman, so she needs an easy-going man.'

'It's a funny day to get married, it's a Sunday. I assume they're coming back here for the wedding?'

'No, no, a wedding on the beach I believe,' said Keith. 'I have to go out there. I've booked my flights, I'm going out to Sydney on Tuesday the ninth and coming back on Tuesday the twenty-third. I don't think I've ever taken a fortnight's holiday before.'

'Two weeks in Australia isn't very long, can't you have a little longer?' He shook his head. 'And will Barbara be travelling out with you, or will she go over there earlier?'

'She's staying over there until after the wedding,' said Keith. 'She says it's not worth coming back and of course she's right. She also wants to help with the wedding plans and she's clearly loving it out there.'

'Goodness,' said Felicity, 'does that mean what I think it means?'

Keith smiled at her. 'I don't know what you're thinking.'

'That you might all end up living over in Australia.'

Keith met her eyes briefly and looked away. 'No,' he said, 'definitely not.'

'Any advance on "no" and "not"?' Felicity asked.

He raised his eyes and this time met her gaze. 'I'm a Cornishman – uproot me and I'd wither and die. I know it's not the county it was, I know a lot of bad things about up-country are creeping down here, but it's my home and I can't ever leave it.' He wanted to add 'and I can't ever leave you', but didn't, couldn't.

Sensing the intensity of his feelings Felicity stood up to break the tension and reached for the kettle. 'Coffee?'

'Yes, please.'

'I'm sure it will work out. Barbara probably doesn't want to stay there permanently and you don't even know Carly and Graham do either.'

'Barbara says they will,' says Keith.

'It must be unsettling with Will in Germany, you're all a bit split up at the moment, aren't you?' Keith nodded. 'I had a period like that when I first came down to Cornwall. Charlie had just died and the children, well, one was in London and one just outside Oxford. It was all very odd after so many years together, but you get used to it.'

'I'm sure I shall,' said Keith. 'My other bit of news is, I'm going to see Miles on Boxing Day.'

'How is he coping with that awful father of his masquerading as his uncle?'

'He's gone,' said Keith.

'The father?'

'No the uncle, the father is dead as you know, the uncle is gone too now, fed up with trying to fill his brother's role, I imagine.'

'Keith, you are the most hopeless liar!' Felicity started to laugh. 'We both know it's the uncle who died, and just look at your face, guilty as charged.'

'My lips are sealed,' said Keith, smiling. 'It's good to see you laugh.'

'Well really, you are useless!' she said. 'Were you always the little boy at school who got picked on by the teachers when they wanted to know what had really happened?'

Keith nodded. 'Yep, that's me.'

'So I'm not going to press you on the subject, it would be unkind, but I hope you find Miles well and happy.'

'I hope so too.' Keith stood up. 'Well, I'd better be going, it's late.'

'Keith before you go, can I tell you something? I know it's not fair to burden you with my boring insecurities but I need someone to talk to and there is no one better than you.'

Keith sat down again and leaning across the table touched her hand. 'Tell me, what's up?'

'I spoke to Jan Shankland on the phone and had a long talk to Adam when I collected my car…'

She paused.

'Go on,' said Keith, encouragingly.

'Sarah came to see me at home when she expressed interest in displaying my work. She did the same with Jan. In both cases she must have spotted our valuable paintings. She asked for a tour of our homes – a major exercise in Jan's case, only taking a second in mine, but enough to see the Constable.'

'And in Adam Mayfield's case, Tom Ward came to his house – obviously thinking he would do better man-to-man, and Adam showed him the Picasso before throwing him out,' Keith said.

'How do you know that?' Felicity asked.

'Because we've taken statements from both Jan and Adam. Because of what you have been through, I told Jack to leave yours until after Christmas. We have plenty of evidence to charge the three of them with a van full of stolen paintings and a dead body, so we won't actually need your statement until a trial date is fixed.'

'Was Christopher Drummond murdered then?' Felicity asked, her voice wobbling slightly.

'Mixed messages. Greg and Tom both went to his house. Greg maintains he hit Christopher but he remained conscious and stumbled backwards over the balcony. Tom reckons Greg pushed him. Either way, the Drummond death was what made them pull out of Cornwall so quickly. Tom and Sarah were in way over their heads in any event. They were in terrible debt, on the verge of bankruptcy and Greg appears to have taken advantage of their desperation. Christopher's death was just too much for them and they appear to be co-operating fully with the police now.'

'The thing is,' said Felicity after a pause, 'I feel so terribly insecure, more so than when Charlie died, I know it's ridiculous.'

'Tell me why?' Keith asked.

'Two things really. Firstly, I have had little or no success selling my paintings until the Windward Gallery appeared to take an interest. Now I know it was just an opportunity to check out the cottage for any possible rich pickings. I feel such an idiot for believing for one minute that my work is any good.'

'You are good, terribly talented,' Keith said. 'Truly, trust me.'

'You're my friend, you would say that but I know it's not true. I really believed that at last I was getting somewhere, and clearly I'm not. It is very depressing.'

'And so all the book illustrations stand for nothing?' Keith asked.

'It's not the same as painting a picture – a one-off – and seeing it sell. I bet you will find all of the paintings Tom and Sarah "sold" of mine, in fact they probably used them as kindling.'

'We are still in the process of a proper inventory but I bet we'll find your paintings, in which case you can sell them to other galleries.'

'No one will want them,' Felicity said.

'This isn't like you – you're always so positive about life. What's going on?'

'That's the second thing,' said Felicity. 'When, in the past, we've been involved in, how shall I put it, "a spot of bother", it has always been over very quickly. This time I had hours and hours on my own to think about life... and death. It's made me question everything. On the one hand, I feel that the experience has taught me that life is for living and we should grab at happiness when and where we can. On the other hand, those long hours have left me fearful of anything, everything. It's why I didn't want to go out tonight.'

'My poor girl,' Keith said. He wanted to touch her, to hold her, but there was a tension building between them which he did not understand but which appeared to be rendering him incapable of movement. He seemed to be holding his breath.

'The thing is, Keith,' Felicity began after a long, tense pause. 'I'm not very good at this, in fact I've never done anything like this before in my whole life, but...' she hesitated, 'stay, please stay.' She did not dare look at him. The silence between them seemed to go on forever. At last she raised her head to see his face so suffused with love and happiness, she did not need him to speak to know his answer.

19

The door was opened by the Irvings' housekeeper. At the sight of Keith, a huge grin appeared on her wonderful ebony face which practically split it in two.

'Why, Chief Inspector,' she said.

'Mary,' said Keith, 'how are you?'

'You remember my name, boy, that's a miracle.'

'Once seen never forgotten,' said Keith, smiling.

'I wasn't very kind to you last time we met, things are different now.'

'I understand, Mary, you were only protecting the people you care for.'

'That's true boy, come this way.'

Keith had forgotten how enormous the Irving house was and how sumptuous. He was shown across the marbled hall through double doors into a vast drawing room. A huge Christmas tree dominated one end of the room and there was a bright fire in the grate. Miles sat on the sofa, his leg stretched out, and Lady Irving was standing by the fireplace.

'Chief Inspector, how very good of you to come, we've been so looking forward to your visit.' She came forward, gracious as ever, and took his hand.

'It's nice to see you again, Lady Irving,' he said, 'and thank you for inviting me.' He turned to Miles and shook his hand. 'You're looking better,' he said.

'Home comforts,' said Miles, smiling warmly at his mother.

'Does he really look better?' Lady Irving enquired, anxiously.

'He certainly does.' Keith looked around him. 'And this room is magnificent, I'd forgotten.'

'Well you've never come on a social call before have you, Chief Inspector.'

'Please,' said Keith, 'call me Keith.'

'Call me Bettine,' Lady Irving replied, though Keith doubted he ever would.

Mary served lunch as a buffet so that Miles did not need to move from the sofa. He could get around on crutches now but was only really comfortable with his leg laid out straight. The meal was delicious; little titbits of smoked salmon and battered prawns in chilli sauce, asparagus and caviar, all washed down with an excellent champagne.

Only when the coffee was served did the conversation turn from trivial matters. 'I understand that Miles has taken you into his confidence,' Lady Irving said. 'You're aware of what has happened both to my husband and to my brother-in-law?'

Keith nodded. Mary had left the room and the door was closed.

'I presume Mary knew who was who?' Keith asked.

Lady Irving smiled. 'Yes, of course.'

'To ask whether you are happy with the outcome is rather a banal question, but I don't know how else to put it,' Keith said.

Lady Irving bowed her elegant head. 'I am content with the outcome. My husband has been very unhappy in the last years, as you can imagine, caged up here pretending to be somebody else. She glanced over at Miles. 'He's not been easy to live with, he'll be happier where he is.'

'Will he really?' said Keith. 'I find it so hard to understand how he became a top industrialist with all the trappings,' he gestured, 'this beautiful house, the champagne lifestyle and all the time he was a communist. What sort of life is he going to lead in Russia, will he cope?'

'Russia is not like it used to be,' Lady Irving said.

'I appreciate that, I know there are some very rich men at the top these days, I just don't understand how the capitalist managed to remain a communist all along.'

'You have to remember,' said Lady Irving, 'that his father was a miner. The family grew up in abject poverty. The reason they did not adopt both twin boys was simply because they could not afford to feed two children. He was very clever, he got a scholarship to Cambridge but a miner's son in those days must have stood out like a sore thumb. He was a quick learner, he learnt how to speak, how to behave, but he was a socialist through and through and he soon caught the attention of the Russian recruitment programme.'

'I think he loved the excitement, too,' said Miles, joining the conversation for the first time.

'How do you mean?' Keith asked.

'He found making money easy, he's super-bright. We've never got on as you know, but I have to acknowledge that about him. I think he probably enjoyed the role of double agent, enjoyed hoodwinking both governments.'

'And getting paid by them both, I expect,' said Lady Irving, smiling, 'to do the same job, knowing him.'

'I'm surprised he didn't get caught out,' said Keith.

'His sort of spying isn't James Bond stuff,' said Miles, 'he's an industrial spy, he wasn't swapping secrets of national security but of technology.'

'Oh, I see,' said Keith, 'I hadn't realised that. I suppose you're right, my idea of a spy is heavily influenced by Ian Fleming.'

There was a silence in the room for a moment and then Lady Irving said. 'There is something I need to tell you, tell you both. I have been putting it off, Miles, because I thought I would wait until Keith was here. I know how much you rely on him as a friend.'

'Oh no,' said Miles, clearly distressed, 'what's happened now? Honestly, Mother, I don't think I can take any more shocks.'

'No, no, it's alright.' She stood up and came and sat on the edge of the sofa, carefully avoiding his damaged leg, and took his hand in hers. 'Your father has another family in Russia, a wife and three children.'

Miles looked profoundly shocked. 'When, how long?'

Lady Irving shrugged elegantly. 'I think he knew her long before he met me. I'm not sure when they married, I know the children are all older than you, older than Elizabeth would have been had she lived.'

'And are they his children by birth or

adoption?'

'By birth,' Lady Irving said gently.

'Would you like me to leave you alone?' Keith said, suddenly feeling very awkward.

'No,' both mother and son said in unison.

'So why did he adopt me then, if he had children of his own?'

'He did it for me,' said Lady Irving. 'It was he and I who stood the risk of producing another child like Elizabeth, he and his Russian wife were fine evidently.'

'What do you think of that then, Chief Inspector?' Miles said, his expression pained. He looked close to tears.

Keith stood up and walked over to the fireplace, turned and faced them both. 'Can I ask you a very personal question?'

Lady Irving nodded. 'You're so wrapped up in our affairs, I think you have every right.'

'How have things been left, financially?'

'Over the last few years Hugo has put everything in my name in trust for Miles.'

'The business, the house, everything?'

'Yes,' she said.

Keith looked at Miles. 'So this child he didn't need to adopt because he had children of his own; this child who disappointed him because he was artistic and musical and wasn't interested in commerce and sport and all the things that Hugo rated; this supposedly unworthy child – he's left his entire fortune to. Everything he's worked for for the whole of his life, he's left to you Miles, though it would have been easy enough to spirit his wealth out of the country with his connections. I am sorry, boy, I think you're just going to have to face it, I think your father loved you.'

They persuaded him to stay the night.

'I'm all packed up,' said Keith, 'I was planning to drive home tonight.'

'To Cornwall?' Lady Irving asked.

'Yes, if I take it slowly, it will be fine.'

'You're mad, it's too far and it's too late,' said Miles.

'Yes, please do stay, don't attempt to drive tonight, we have plenty of rooms made up,' Lady Irving insisted.

He protested weakly and gave in. He fetched his bag from the car and Mary showed him to the most sumptuous en suite bedroom. When he returned to the drawing room, the cushions had been plumped up, the fire loaded with fresh logs and wine had been poured.

'I'm going to leave you boys to it,' Lady Irving said. 'I'm going to go to bed and watch some trashy Boxing Day television.'

'I don't see you and trashy Boxing Day television being natural bed fellows, if I may say so,' Keith suggested.

'You'd be surprised,' said Lady Irving, 'the trashier the better. I adore *Eastenders* and especially *The X Factor*.'

'Good Lord,' said Keith.

Lady Irving kissed him on the cheek. 'Thank you for coming, you've been an invaluable help to this family and a true friend to my son.'

'You have a son to be proud of,' said Keith, 'but don't for God's sake tell him or he'll become unbearably pompous.' They smiled indulgently at Miles who attempted to look embarrassed.

They ate a delicious chicken and rice dish prepared by Mary around the fire and then at Miles's insistence Keith helped them to an Armagnac each.

'She's a good woman, your mother,' Keith said. Miles nodded. 'Have you got over all your difficulties?'

'She is always going to feel guilty about Marianna,' said Miles, 'and there is nothing I can do to help her with that. She shouldn't have split us up but my father is a bully. He didn't want two children and she had to go along with it, I accept that. She loves me, I love her, and we've been through a lot together. She is the only mother I'm ever going to have and I'm her only child – we're fine.'

'I'm glad,' said Keith, and raised his glass towards Miles.

'Anya is coming to stay next week.'

'Really?' said Keith. That's wonderful.'

'She was very nervous about coming back to London, she hasn't been here since…' Miles's voice trailed away. 'But I have explained that while Notting Hill is very near Paddington, it is rather different.'

'It's certainly that,' said Keith.

'So I plan to show her everything – Buckingham Palace, the Changing of the Guard, the Tower of London and Carnaby Street, everything.'

'How will you do that?' said Keith, nodding towards his leg.

'By taxi.'

'Of course, I keep forgetting that you're a wealthy man.'

'I'm not going to let it go to my head. I only have to think of Harry and Becky and how lucky I am to have survived that car crash. They were young and happy and full of life and were snuffed out just like that – and I survived, why me?'

'Oh Lord, you're not suffering from survivor's

guilt as well as everything else?' Keith asked, smiling.

'In a way, yes. I always seem to be a survivor. Look at me and my sister, I was saved from the orphanage and then saved again from that terrible man who murdered her. How I see it is this. If I've been lucky enough to have got this far, then I must use the wealth I will inherit and the privileges I have, to do some good in the world. I've been thinking of taking my musical talents, such as they are, to Romania – maybe set up some children's orchestras, that sort of thing. I've got a mate at college, he's a really talented pianist, he's all up for joining me.'

'That sounds like a great idea,' said Keith, 'but don't spend your whole life thinking that you're obliged to pay back. Use your money to help charities, of course, do what you can for your country of birth, in particular for her children, but remember to enjoy life too. Find a nice girl, marry her, raise some children, enjoy the simple things – that's the best thing you can do to honour the memory of Becky and Harry and above all Marianna, and that is what they would want for you, above everything.'

'Do you think I stand a chance with Anya?' Miles asked.

'I don't know,' said Keith, honestly, 'but be

careful, don't take on more than you can cope with. She is carrying a lot of baggage, so are you. A relationship between you could be wonderfully healing for you both, or open wounds that simply will not heal.'

Miles nodded. 'You're quite a wise old owl, you know that? Anyway, enough of me. How are you, how have you managed this Christmas being somewhat orphaned yourself, Chief Inspector?'

'Oh strange, not unpleasant. Today has been great, of course, and I had a good time with my sister. We rang Australia yesterday, they had a barbecue on the beach, would you believe.'

'It's what they do Down Under.'

'I know,' said Keith, 'it just doesn't seem right.'

'You're really not into this whole Australian thing, are you?' Miles said, laughing.

Keith shook his head. 'It looks like my daughter and her future husband are going to stay there permanently and my wife loves Sydney and the lifestyle. Before I know it, they'll be suggesting we all emigrate out there, I can see it coming.'

'Would that be such a bad thing? I know you're dreading retirement, it would be a new challenge.'

'I can't leave Cornwall,' Keith said, taking a sip of Armagnac and staring into the fire.

Miles regarded him shrewdly. 'It's not just Cornwall you can't leave, is it?'

Keith looked up at him, startled. 'What makes you say that?'

'Oh, come off it,' said Miles, 'I'm not the great student of human nature you are, Chief Inspector, but I can see it in your face – it's not just Cornwall you can't leave, there is *someone* you can't leave.'

The wine, which had flowed on and off all day, the warmth of the fire and the easy relationship he had with this boy all combined to loosen Keith's inhibitions. He needed to tell someone, and it seemed to be the right moment and the right person.

'There is someone,' he said, 'I love her very much, more than I have ever loved anyone, but...'

'But you have a responsibility to your wife and children.'

'Yes,' said Keith, still gazing into the fire.

'You're a wise man, Chief Inspector, you'll do the right thing when the time comes.'

'I do hope so, Miles,' said Keith, 'I do hope so.'

EPILOGUE

Saturday January 9, 2010, St Ives, Cornwall

Chief Inspector Keith Penrose strode up the street, fished a key out of his pocket and opened the purple door to Jericho Cottage. Harvey came roaring down the stairs, yelping with excitement and threw himself at Keith's legs.

'Good morning, boy,' he said, 'glad to see someone is pleased to see me.'

'I'm pleased to see you,' said Felicity from the top of the stairs.

'Well, I don't see you bounding down the stairs, yelping for joy,' Keith said.

'You do ask rather a lot of a girl, Chief Inspector.'

Keith in response came up the stairs two at a time, took her in his arms and kissed her very thoroughly.

At last she extricated herself. 'Harvey and I were just going for a walk on the beach, do you want to come?'

'I do,' said Keith, 'but before that there is someone I would like you to meet. I have one duty call to make before I have the rest of the day off, though I have to say it's hardly a duty.'

'So where are we going?' said Felicity.

'Nosey, wait and see.'

Five minutes later they were outside the door of Violet Symonds' flat. Keith rang the bell.

'I think you should at least tell me...' Felicity began.

'Ssh, wait and see, so impatient!' They waited a long time.

'Shouldn't you ring the bell again?' Felicity asked.

'No,' said Keith, 'it takes her a long while to get to the front door.' As he spoke the door opened. Violet looked first at Keith and then at Felicity and then spotted Harvey.

'Oh, what a dear, come here, pet, let me have a look at you.' Harvey obligingly walked into the house, tail wagging. 'Come with Aunty Violet and she'll give you a biscuit.' Felicity and Keith followed Violet down the narrow passage to her kitchen.

'Is this...' Felicity whispered.

'I said ssh,' said Keith.

They arrived in the kitchen; Violet already

had her hand in the biscuit barrel and was beginning to feed Harvey little titbits.

'Jack told me you were very fond of dogs so I thought you'd like it if we brought Harvey on a visit,' Keith said.

'He told you, did he? He is such a nice young man, your sergeant, told me all about his baby daughter, photographs and everything. Let me get you some tea.'

'No,' said Keith, 'I have something to tell you first, Violet.'

She looked up at him expectantly and Felicity immediately caught the look of fear in her face, but Keith was not going to prolong Violet's agony. 'It's over, Violet. I've been advised that no charges are going to be brought either against you or your son. It's finished, you can move on.'

Violet burst into tears. Felicity quickly reached her side and guided her to a chair. Harvey, worried, put his paws up on her knee.

'I can't believe it,' she said, 'I can't believe it after all these years.'

'I'll make some tea,' Felicity said.

Keith sat down beside Violet and took her hand. 'Truly Violet, it's at an end, you can at last put this behind you.'

'Have you told Andy?'

'I haven't,' said Keith, 'but I will if you want

284

me to. I rather thought you might like to do it.'

'I would, dear, that was very thoughtful of you.' She fished around up her sleeve, found a handkerchief, dried her eyes and blew her nose. 'I'm sorry about this, it was just such a relief, thank you for coming to tell me. Now who is this lovely young lady?'

'Hardly young,' said Felicity, 'my name is Felicity Paradise, I'm a neighbour of yours. I live just around the corner and this hound you are spoiling to death is Harvey.'

They drank the tea Felicity had prepared and chatted. 'Do you think this will make relationships easier with your son and his family?' Keith asked.

'I hope so, I hope it's not too late but nothing is going to change the attitude of the stuck-up bitch.'

'That's her daughter-in-law,' Keith translated, with a smile.

'Well she is, dear, there is no other way to put it. However, the thing that kept Andy and I apart was our dreadful secret and now that it is over, I think maybe we can be friends again and maybe I'll get to know the children.'

'I do hope so,' said Keith, 'you deserve some happiness, Violet.'

'I'm alright,' she said, 'but I'd feel a lot better if you'd bring this little dog to see me sometimes. I was telling your Jack, I had a dog throughout my childhood, but David didn't like them and now I'm just too old.'

'What about a cat?' Felicity suggested.

'I've got an old cat, rules the place, hates me really. I'm a dog person, which I expect he knows.'

'Of course I'll bring Harvey round to see you,' Felicity promised, 'he's certainly taken to you.' Harvey had jumped up onto Violet's lap and was sitting there as if they had known each other for ever.

'I'm afraid our relationship is all about the biscuits,' said Violet sagely, and they all laughed.

As they were leaving, Felicity and Harvey walking ahead down the passage towards the front door, Violet tugged at Keith's sleeve.

'I like your young lady,' she said in a stage whisper, 'hang onto her, she's a good'un.'

Keith smiled at her a little sadly. 'I'll try,' he said.

They walked the round of St Ives, across Porthmeor beach, around the Island, across Porthgwidden and onto Harbour beach. The tide was out, the sun was shining, they walked right out to the sea. Harvey was in seventh heaven, dragging about dead fish that were almost as big as him and growling ferociously.

'He's going to smell awful when we get home,' said Felicity. They turned as they reached the water's edge and looked back at the town. The sun glinted on Porthminster Beach Café, making it stand out in startling white against the yellow sand; their gaze swept across the higgledy-piggledy cottages and streets, the church, the lifeboat, the harbour, the Sloop, the pier.

'What do you think when you see all this?' Keith asked.

'Home,' said Felicity, without hesitation.

'Truly?'

She nodded.

'Ever since we met I've always been afraid that one day you would fly back to Oxford.'

Felicity shook her head. 'No, this is my home now.'

'I'm glad.' He took her hand and they began to retrace their steps towards the Wharf. Keith whistled for Harvey and he appeared around the corner of a fishing boat with a large, very dead fish in his mouth.

'Oh, yuck,' they both chorused.

'Four weeks and two days until I fly to Australia,' Keith said, with a heavy heart.

'You do know, don't you,' said Felicity, 'I'm not expecting this to last, Keith. You're married, you have children and the prospect of grandchildren. I know this is just a fleeting moment in our lives, very precious, very special, but I know at some point reality has to kick in, which in our case is going to be in four weeks' time.'

'I don't know what to say, I don't know what to do, I don't know how things will be until I get out there,' said Keith.

'Is Will flying with you?' Keith nodded. 'He may love it out there, too. There must be a mass of opportunity for ship-building, I would think. It's a country for the young, and with his sister there...' she took a deep breath, 'maybe you should all stay over there.'

'I've told you, I can't. Let's not talk about it, I can't bear it.'

An uneasy silence fell between them as they reached the Wharf. Felicity attached Harvey's lead and managed to persuade him to leave his precious fish behind. They climbed up the steep steps of Mount Zion and headed up through the twisting streets.

Suddenly, Felicity stopped in her tracks. 'Keith.'

'Yes,' he said, turning to her, his face creased with anxiety.

'You're right; let's not waste any time agonising. We have four weeks. Let's make these four weeks the best weeks of our lives. No thoughts of the future, no doubts from the past, just live for now.'

He smiled at her, his love for her there for all the world to see. 'I think that's a very good idea, Mrs Paradise.'

He took her hand and led her up the last few steps and through the purple door of Jericho Cottage.

Acknowledgements
I would particularly like to thank Dr Lucy Mackillop,
Diana Palmer, Sally Gibert, Jo Pearce, Heather & Ivan
Corbett and Kate Richards and my family for their
remarkable understanding at being so severely neglected
during the writing of this book.